THE DAVID CHRONICLES

Volume II

A Peek at Bathsheba

USA Today
Bestselling Author

UVI POZNANSKY

This novel can be read as a standalone novel, as well as a part of The David Chronicles, a trilogy in the voice of David, describing his youth, prime of life, and old age: Rise to Power A Peek at Bathsheba The Edge of Revolt

Published by Uviart
P.O. Box 3233 Santa Monica CA 90408
Blog: uviart.blogspot.com
Email: uvi.author@gmail.com

First Edition 2014
Printed in the United States of America
Book design, cover image and design by
Uvi Poznansky

ISBN: 978-0-9849932-7-7
ASIN: B00LEPPDV6

Contents

Prologue

A long time ago I used to think that my youth was to blame for failing to understand my wives. No longer can I use that excuse, because I know all too well, there is no youth in me anymore. Which leaves me as baffled as ever, especially when it comes to the one woman I adore: Bathsheba.

When I catch her scent, or even when I imagine it, something in me turns to liquid. Then, trying to harden my heart and remove her from my mind I find myself confused, and the rage in me intensifies, perhaps because I cannot remember the last time I have seen her. Alas, the distance between us seems to expand in so many ways with each passing year.

So imagine my surprise this morning, when I wake up to the soft sound of her footfalls, which makes me turn my eyes to the wall to try, to catch sight of her reflection. There it is, moving fluidly across the blade, the wide, polished blade of Goliath's sword which is hung in my chamber, right here over my head.

First Bathsheba throws open the window, letting in a cold morning breeze. As if to tell me that this is already autumn, a smell of dry leaves wafts in. The silk curtains start swishing as they sway, they billow wildly around her, blotting and redrawing the curves of her silhouette, which in a blink, brings back to me the fullness of her figure back then, when she was expecting our first child. I remember the way I held her in my arms that hot summer evening, right there by that window. Together, we looked out at the last glimmer of the sun, sinking.

I remember the way she guided my hand, ever so gently, so I could feel her skin, her warmness, and the faint kick of the baby inside her.

Then the glow dimmed, it smoldered into darkness. After a while we could no longer guess the exact place where it had happened.

Now, looking at her back from across the chamber, I wonder: does she remember that moment? And if so, does she remember it fondly? Is there a glint of laughter playing in her eyes?

The rings, high up there above her head, start squealing as she slides the curtain, with a harsh movement, across its pole. A moment later she comes over here and bends over the bed, where the young girl, Abishag, lays dreaming, with her arms loosely wrapped around me.

"Get up," Bathsheba says to her, without bothering to look at me, to check if I am awake. "I've brought fresh towels for you. Get up."

The girl opens her eyes and at once, her muscles tense up. She withdraws from me and with a light-footed leap hops off the bed. I can tell she is embarrassed, because this has been her first night here, with me, and because it must be hard to decide what to do next: walk backwards from my wife and shrink away, somehow—or curtsey before her, which is an awkward thing to do when you are wearing next to nothing.

"Go already, go wash yourself," says Bathsheba, looking at the girl with an amused, belittling smile on her lips. "You should've cleaned yourself last night, before coming to *his* bed. Didn't they tell you?"

Unable to utter a word, the girl shakes her head, No. Now she clasps the set of towels to her bare chest, heaves a little sigh and scurries out the door.

Meanwhile I raise my eyes to my wife, feeling too frail to prop myself up on the pillow. With most people, except sometimes with her, I must change my speech, make it different than the language of my thoughts, because I do not wish to sound too lofty, too poetic, too removed from everyday discourse.

"Don't talk about me as if I'm not here," I tell her, hearing the shiver, the old age in my voice. "I hate it when you do that. Makes me feel as if I'm nothing more than air."

Bathsheba says nothing, but somehow I can read her mind, I know what she is thinking. "Air? No, quite the contrary: you're much heavier than that. At this stage of the game, you're a burden."

Becoming irate I go on to demand, "I'm still the king, am I not? My name is praised throughout the kingdom. So in my presence I suggest you use it."

Unexpectedly, Bathsheba decides to relent. "I'll do better than that, David," she says. "I'll come to your bed."

"You will?"

"Yes," she says, and her voice takes on a sweet, seductive tone, the way I remember it from the old days, the days of our passion. "Right here, see? I hope you still have some strength in you."

At hearing this, my lungs expand. Suddenly I can breathe easier, the pounding of my heart quickens, and the chill releases some of its grip on me. It is much more bearable than before. So I toss away the blankets and make room for her.

Taking her time she grabs the corner of the satin sheet and starts to remove it, perhaps because in it she senses the fragrance that the girl has left here.

There is a catch in my throat as I whisper, "Come closer, Bathsheba, my love."

Instead, she curls herself away from me, at the other edge of the mattress, and by her silence I guess she has too much to say.

Even so, my old heart skips a beat, because all of a sudden I recall how she used to laugh, with no restraint, in my arms. Perhaps, like me, she has not forgotten how I would swirl the rosy wine in my goblet, take in the sweet, intoxicating aroma, and instead of sipping I would tip it over her belly, and let it drizzle all across the rosy blush of her skin.

Between one lick and another I would murmur to her, "Oh Bathsheba."

And in my happiness I would later write, "*Your graceful legs are like jewels, the work of an artist's hands. Your navel is a rounded goblet that never lacks blended wine.*"

Now, despite the weakness in my knees I rise up, and make my way around the bed and kneel there before her in my most gallant manner, which is when I catch sight of the dark circles under her eyes. Perhaps, like me, she has had a sleepless night.

It is then that I start suspecting, for the first time, that there must be a reason, a clear purpose in her mind for coming here.

"Bathsheba," I whisper, opening my arms to her. "I need you."

Her hand is trembling a bit as she fumbles to bring out a small papyrus roll tucked there, under her velvet belt. "Let's stop playing games," she says, tersely. "Seriously, look here. This is a matter that truly demands your attention."

At the risk of turning the conversation in an unwanted direction, "How boring," I complain. "I can't stand matters that demand my attention. They're never any fun, are they? At best, I find them oppressive."

"Listen to me," she says, shaking the thing in front of my face to make it crackle, just like those crisp leaves flying out there outside my window. "This here," she stresses, "it's a matter of life and death."

"I don't want to hear it, not now," say I. "Such matters, overblown as they invariably are, become trivial when you find yourself as close to dying as I am. The time that remains to me is waning, so let's not waste the moment. It is too precious, my love."

"You're losing yourself in dreams when the time is for action," she says, doing her best to contain the growing irritation in her voice.

And when I do not respond, she adds, "I wouldn't have come to you if this were just a minor upset, in some God forsaken place out there, in the far reaches of the land. But now, this is different. It's happening here, close to home. If you make the mistake of ignoring it, if you keep your eyes closed, the throne may be toppled."

"Nonsense." I wave my hand in the manner of dismissal, which in a blink, makes tears well in her eyes.

She lowers her voice. "It's not just my life that's in danger—but the life of my son, too. I mean, our son. Please, David, hear me out—"

"You know how bored I've become with politics," I say. "Poetry is what I wish to hear."

"Oh," says she, gathering her skirt and getting up. "What was I thinking, coming here to talk to you."

So I search for a way to appease her. "Your voice," I say, "is so lovely, so full of drama, especially when you're angry. I wouldn't mind listening to you reading something else to me, something lyrical and inspiring. Oh, I know! How about one of my psalms? Would you read it for me, Bathsheba?"

All she gives me is silence, so I press on. "You used to adore my way with words."

"I did," she says, almost agreeably, "until the moment came when you lost me, lost my admiration."

I cannot help crying, "What! When did that happen?"

In turn she bristles at me, "When you wrote those words, those awful, hateful words that made me learn, once and for all, what you are."

Taken aback I try not to betray any sign of hurt feelings. None of my other wives has ever dared to tell me that anything I wrote was less than perfect. None of them has ever offered any type of literary critique, let alone hinted that my work was, in any way, objectionable. But then again, Bathsheba is unlike Michal, Ahinoam, Abigail, Maachah, Haggith, Abital, and Eglah. They are mine. She is not.

From the beginning I hungered for her, perhaps because she belonged to another. The sweetest taste belongs to the stolen apple. Yet I cannot figure out why, over the years, this taste has soured.

"Those words, they've stuck in my mind," she says, acidly.

I try, as best I can, to swallow my pride. Having failed at that, I demand, "Words? What words are you talking about?"

"Don't you know?"

"Of course not!"

"Men," she sighs.

"Is it something I wrote recently?"

"No. You wrote it decades ago."

I throw my hands in the air. "Women!"

We stare at each other.

Finally I mutter, "You could've said something to me a decade or two earlier, couldn't you?"

Embarrassed, she looks away. "No, how could I?" she asks. "At the time, I held myself back from complaining. I made it my mission to find favor in your eyes."

"What a tease you are, Bathsheba. No woman is better than you at stoking the flames of desire."

"For the sake of my son—I mean, your son—I had to establish my position in the palace."

"Establish yourself you did, quite brilliantly," say I.

"It wasn't an easy thing, climbing all the way up to the top, with so many girls down there, in the royal harem, and on this floor—all your wives, who had given you so many children before you came to know me."

"Ambition is something I understand."

"Yes. It's something we share, you and I."

"What I don't understand is this: how could you go on holding a grudge, holding it for so many years, over some petty psalm I wrote."

She shrugs.

"Words," she says at last, "have power."

"Well, will you tell me now? What, in heavens name, did I say that was so offensive to you?"

"Ah." She waves her hand. "Forget it. What does it matter, now."

But I insist. "It matters to me."

So she takes a deep breath, and from memory she recites, quite fluidly, "*Psalm of David, when Nathan the prophet came to him, after he had gone in to Bathsheba*—"

"Oh, that!" I exclaim, with great excitement. I hold myself back from saying, "What an inspired psalm, if I say so myself!"

But by her little smile it seems that she can hear my thoughts. Bathsheba rolls her eyes, as if to say, "Yeah, right."

"What d'you have against it? This psalm was highly acclaimed, I mean, everyone agreed it ranked up there, at the top of my published work. They called it a prayer, a conversation with God, because it expressed a sense of repentance that is deeper and more meaningful, perhaps, than any sins I may have committed."

She smiles at me, acidly. "Then, you recite it."

So with my usual flair I deliver what I consider to be my finest lines. "*Against You, You only, I have sinned, and done what is evil in Your sight, so that You are justified when You speak, and blameless when You judge.*"

"There," says Bathsheba. "You see?"

"See what?"

"How you never find it in your heart to take responsibility for your actions."

"What? Weren't you listening? Didn't I confess, quite profusely and with such a lovely, catchy rhythm, before the Lord?"

"What does He have to do with this?" She shakes her head in disbelief. "What about the shame I suffered all over town, the nasty talk that followed me everywhere, the evil wishes cast against my unborn child? You sinned against me, and most of all, against my husband, Uriah, yet you never expressed any remorse to me, nor did you ask forgiveness of him, before sending him to his death."

"Really, Bathsheba, how could I? Admitting my weaknesses is not in my nature. I am, after all, the king."

"Exactly," she says, seething now. "That's what you are: a king pretending to repent—but refusing to ask forgiveness, or gratify anyone but an unseen God. The real victims don't matter, do they."

In place of an answer I shuffle uneasily from one knee to another.

"So now, David, get up," she says. "What's the use of kneeling before me, when you never say the right words."

I find it hard to admit, "I wish I knew what to tell you."

"Figure it out," says she, "before it's too late."

To which I beg, "Help me, love."

"Forget love," says Bathsheba, coldly. "It's what got me in trouble in the first place."

*

Quite abruptly she rises from my bed, flings the door wide open and leaves me—but not before turning around to toss the papyrus scroll with great fury in my direction.

The thing flaps, flips, and flutters in the air, until coming to a rest up here on the wall, hanging by a thread over the hilt of Goliath's sword. Reflected in reverse across the surface of the blade, its letters seem as foreign as Egyptian hieroglyphs.

I am old, too old to learn a new language. What is written here bears no meaning to me.

The door slams shut, and from the other side of it I hear the thud of her footsteps. Away she goes, stomping across the corridor with pronounced anger.

"Come back," I whisper, fearing that there is no one around this place to hear me.

And just when I crawl under the blankets, and turn my face to the wall, getting ready for the chill to take me back in its grip, I hear her footfalls coming back. The door is still closed between us, which muffles her voice when she cries out, "Help you want? You'll get it when you give it."

"I wish I knew what you want me to do," I mumble, sinking into my pillow.

Which is the moment I sense, by the cold draft on the back of my neck, that she has opened the door, if only by a crack.

"Perhaps," says Bathsheba, "you can't do it anymore, you can't find the words to reach out to me."

She waits a moment for a reply, which I am too sleepy to give. My eyes are heavy, and the only thing I can still discern is shadows, dancing on the wall. Without having to look I sense a new presence. There it is, in the corner.

Slumber is here, waiting.

Bathsheba comes closer and this time, she kneels before me. "Perhaps asking forgiveness is a hard thing, too hard for you to do. That," she says, "I can understand. But rising to action was something you used to enjoy, and you did it quite well, especially when threatened."

"Yes," I murmur, in a tone that grows more and more sluggish, from one word to the next. "I used to thrive on it. Fame... Grandeur... Glory... "

The last thing I sense before sleep comes is her touch. She clasps my hand, and with her warmest voice she says, "I beg you: show me you still care. Read the scroll. Do it now, David, because this you must realize: my life, and the life of our son, are both in grave danger."

I Am A King

Chapter 1

I am a king. Truly, I am!

At first I find it hard to believe, and I wipe my eyes in wonder, and try to convince myself of this puzzling fact, because when you dream about ascending to the throne for as long as I have, you learn to suspect what you see, because it may still be the lingering effect of your fantasy, even if to you it seems real.

Of course I have no throne to speak of, not yet, because I cannot inherit anything that belonged to my predecessor. Alas, my kingdom is limited to a small, insignificant province, I mean, to the territory of my own tribe, Judea. The elders of Israel, who represent the other eleven tribes, show no signs of accepting my rule. They insist that to them I am a criminal, a traitor who joined forces with the enemy. They are unreasonably stubborn, which forces us into a bloody, unnecessary civil war. Are they blind? Can't they see how much easier it would be for all concerned, had they relented?

It is my goal—illusive as it may be—to minimize our casualties. This goal keeps me out of reach of Saul's court, and his property. I don't mind steering clear of it, because after all, not much is left. The House of Saul has collapsed. His palace is in ruins, its contents looted by our people as well as the Philistines.

Since his defeat at Mount Gilboa, not a single piece of furniture has been recovered and brought here from his court, which matters little to me. My taste is more refined, and much more expensive than his.

Immediately following my hasty coronation in the city of Hebron I find myself so bored with military skirmishes as to delegate the pleasure of fighting to my first in command, Joav. Which gives me the luxury of turning my attention to what I enjoy most: beauty. My secret pleasure—besides women—is creating the loveliest throne room plunder can buy.

So this morning I sharpen my quill and begin writing a message to the renowned craftsmen in the Phoenician city of Sidon, north of the border. They are experts at producing dyes, by means of breaking the shells of tens of thousands of sea snails to extract a precious gram of pigment, which must be prevented from degrading in the sun, and tended to with the utmost care, for which only they know the secret, having perfected it over many years.

This skill, combined with their unequaled art of embroidery, is just what I need for embellishing the decor in this place. I would pay any price for that bluish purple indigo dye, because it is so rare as to become the mark of royalty.

I must persuade them, with just the right phrases, to come here to my compound, in this God forsaken minor province, and take measurements for curtains, pillows, armrests and other fineries. No one would be better than them at the task of adorning this place with exotic fabrics, so it may look fit for the ruler of a future empire.

To my dismay I find it impossible to set my mind on my composition, because as a married man I must attend, first and foremost, to the needs of my family. Taking care of one woman is difficult enough. Multiply that triple fold, and you will come close to understanding what I am going through. Clamoring for my attention, here come my precious sweethearts.

"A new decor would be nice, my lord. Truly, I have nothing against it," says my wife, Abigail. "But how about a personal gift, I mean, a little something for your servant? A purple dress? Wouldn't it look deliciously attractive on me?"

And when I say nothing, she goes on to promise, "It'll make me be good, so good to you, in ways you've never even imagined before, which in turn may inspire my lord to write something new, perhaps a psalm for your servant, to be admired by all of us here, and by every cultured person in the entire country."

She always peppers her talk with *my lord* and *your servant*, which is pleasant to hear most of the time, but at this particular moment I find it somewhat overbearing.

So in turn I yawn, which prevents me from thinking of a quick way to brush her off.

To remind me how much I love her, Abigal quotes my best lines, which I wrote for her at the beginning of our affair. "*My beloved is mine and I am his,*" she breathes in my ear. "*He browses among the lilies. Until the day breaks, and the shadows flee. Turn, my beloved, and be like a gazelle, or like a young stag on the rugged hills.*"

I have to admit, "That's a pretty good line, if I say so myself! It has become so famous as to be claimed by every man in the land as his own."

Before I can go back to my writing, my other wife, Ahinoam of Jezreel, leans over my desk with her newborn baby. With motherly pride she bounces him this way and that in her arms.

"You know me," she says. "Unlike that other wife of yours I'm modest, much too modest to ask anything for myself."

"Thank goodness," say I, with a sigh of relief.

"But then again, what about your son, Amnon?"

"What about him?"

"He's your first born, dear, the fruit of your loins," she says, with a sudden blush.

"I suppose he is," say I. "So?"

Ahinoam puts Amnon in my arms, wanting me to coo at him. "I don't want to put any ideas in your head," she says, "but—"

"Then, don't!"

"But, but won't he look adorable, and ever so princely, in a cute little purplish suit?"

"I'm too busy for chitchat, don't you see?" I tell her, trying to subdue the tone of complaint in my voice.

"But—"

"And," I go on to say, "adorable as he may be, I'm not going to squander my hard earned booty, and on top of it let tens of thousands of sea snails be crushed into extinction, just for a trifle, for a baby suit, which he'll soon outgrow."

"That would be such a waste," says Abigail, nudging Ahinoam, ever so gently, away from me. "On the other hand, if you'd find it in your heart to buy your servant a new gown, I promise: I'm never going to outgrow it!"

"Oh darling," says Ahinoam, under her breath. "It would be quite a challenge to get any bigger than you already are."

Which Abigail pretends not to hear. Batting her eyelashes, she blows a little kiss in my direction and says, "The expense is well worth it, my lord. Really, it's just like saving money."

Meanwhile, my new bride, Maacha, elbows her way between both of them. "Splurging is something I truly appreciate," she says, "but why would you do it for simple women, women who don't have a drop of royal blood flowing in their veins? They're commoners. I'm not!"

To which I say, "I have nothing against commoners. I'm one of them."

Abigail smiles. "Thank you, my lord."

At that, Maacha stamps her foot. "Did you hear that? She admits being a maid. I'm a princess!"

And Ahinoam jeers at her, "Who cares? You're not even one of us, are you?"

"Enough already," say I. "Take leave of me, all of you."

Instead, Maacha makes her way into my arms and from here, she hisses at the other two, long and hard, in a manner that is questionably regal.

To placate her I try murmuring sweet nothings in her ear. "*Your lips drop sweetness as the honeycomb, my bride, milk and honey are under your tongue. The fragrance of your garments is like the fragrance of Lebanon.*"

"Forget milk and honey," she bristles at me. "And forgive me for saying so, I don't care much for poetry, either."

"Really? You don't? That," I say, "is a problem. Any wife of mine must appreciate the finer things in life—"

"What I really need right now is one thing," says Maacha. "A purple veil for the upcoming wedding. I want to look mysterious."

I hesitate to refuse her, so she presses on. "Need I say the obvious? By marrying me, you're about to gain an important political ally. My father, the honorable king Talmai of Geshur, will be ready to attack your enemies from their back when you face them in battle."

"My enemies," say I, "are my brethren."

"Even so. Ours is a union of mutually calculated benefits. You give, I take."

"Is that how it works?"

"It is," she replies. "So why not treat me in the manner to which I'm accustomed? Spoil me, David, with your gifts, your little tokens of luxury."

I shake my head in dismay. "Why, no! I'm not going to ask for your father's help to spill the blood of my brethren, just so you can dye your veil purple."

"Soldiers are expendable," says Maacha, in a perfectly calm voice. "Not so us women."

"My lord," says Abigail, "if you don't treat us with proper care, we may start suspecting that the rumors are true."

Noting that the three of them are exchanging glances I take a step back. "Rumors?"

"Dear," says Ahinoam, "are you cheating on us?"

"Who, me?"

"Tell us the truth," she demands. "Are you having an affair? Tongues are wagging all over town, about those two new girls next door, Abital and Eglah."

So what choice do I have but to swear, "In heaven's name, what are you suggesting?"

"I'm not suggesting," says she. "I'm just saying."

"I would never betray my wives!"

"Wouldn't you, dear?"

I clap my hand over my heart, most earnestly, and in an offended tone I say, "Of course not! Which is why I've already proposed to both of them."

"I see," says Maacha.

Abigail giggles. "I can just imagine, my lord, what words you used."

"Yeah," says Ahinoam, and with a hint of mockery in her tone she quotes the line I once whispered in her ear, and in the ear of any other girl I knew, "*Your eyes behind your veil are doves. Your hair is like a flock of goats, descending from the hills of Gilead.*"

Taking a cue from her, Abigail goes on to quote my next line, "*Your lips are like a scarlet ribbon. Your mouth is lovely. Your temples behind your veil are like the halves of a pomegranate.*"

And Maacha says, "I don't really care for all that agricultural talk. A purple veil is what I want. Give it to me and then, who cares? You can describe me as any kind of fruit you wish."

"None of you women understand me!" I cry. "All this pressure is for no better reason than getting a dab of indigo dye, which I assure you, I'll use for one purpose, and one only: to make this place the pinnacle of elegance, so that anyone who visits here will know, at a single glance, that I am not merely a tribal king—but one headed for imperial power."

How long, Lord, how long? How much nagging can a man take from his wives? I throw my hands up, and with an indignant air I fling the door, leaving a royal slam behind me.

*

"Domestic unrest has its rewards," says Joav, my first in command, when I tell him about the contentious joy I get from my wives.

I raise an eyebrow, as if to ask, "Really? And what rewards might those be?"

"One of them," he says, "is having a little fun on the side. You're so lucky to have a growing collection of young, beautiful maidens, who are only too happy to please you, and to listen to your complaints about the institution of marriage."

"But," say I, "before long they, too, expect me to marry them. I'm bored to death."

"Ha! Boredom never killed anyone," says he. "And you have this to consider: the most accurate measure for prestige is how many wives a king has, and the size of his harem."

I refrain from telling him that the constant search for new girls is driven not by boredom but rather by desire, my secret desire for a woman I cannot have. I thought I saw a reflection of her, one steamy evening, on the roof directly below my tower.

There she was, bathing.

How vividly I recall her outline, the way it took shape out of the mist that was whirling, twisting, rising whiff by swirly whiff from the surface of the water. I close my eyes, the better to imagine how she looked. A rosy sunset light played upon her neck, her ears, her cheeks, revealing a hot blush that was tempered with sweet air.

Until that moment I had thought there was no such thing as burning with desire, except perhaps in literary exaggerations, in poetry. Oh how wrong had I been!

With this woman presenting herself to my imagination in such an alluring way, I began worrying that I would surely go down in history as a sinner. Truly I wished to stay honest with the public—but knew I would find it difficult to do so. Being absolutely frank about the naughty thoughts in my head would surely prevent me from looking good in their eyes.

Attempting to balance these two goals—honesty and striving to be wholesome—would force me to instruct my scribes to omit some details, and to obscure others behind a pile of truth.

Since then she has disappeared. I sat by that window every evening, and waited. I waited until the stars came out, until the horizon would reveal the first, hesitant hint of sunrise. All in vain. I never saw her again. Only a dove here, a dove there would flutter from time to time across that roof, and come to a perch on the rolled edge of her porcelain tub, which is bone dry now, and collecting dust.

In her absence I have made up my mind to stop thinking about her, stop imagining her shadow opening to me out of every corner.

Instead I should focus on other things, such as ruling, studying the law, and trying to uphold it, which is a complicated task for me, especially because of one particular commandment. "*You shall not covet your neighbor's house. You shall not covet your neighbor's wife, or his manservant or maidservant, his ox or donkey, or anything that belongs to your neighbor.*"

I find it interesting that a neighbor's wife is likened, in our culture, to his ox or donkey. If I were a woman, which—thank God!—I am not, I would riot in the streets over this. Being who I am, I keep arguing with myself—without becoming entirely convinced—that the prohibition of coveting may be reasonable, but it applies to all but me, because after all I own everything everyone else owns.

Am I not a king?

Joav smirks under his thick mustache. When in public, he knows to shrink behind me, never stirring out of my shadow, so I may claim his victories on the battlefield as mine. He is quiet then, barely noticeable. Not so now.

"I can see," he says, a bit too brazenly for my taste, "that you live in a world of your own. Your happy family, such as it is, distracts you from other pressing matters."

"Such as?"

"You sure you want to hear?"

"Why shouldn't I?"

"Because," he says, "handling bad news is something you can—if you so wish—delegate to me."

I glower at him. "How can I delegate anything," say I, "about which I know absolutely nothing? Go ahead already, tell me."

"All right," says Joav, twiddling the wiry ends of his mustache. "This is the latest development. Abner son of Ner, the commander of what remains of Saul's army, has taken Ish-Bosheth son of Saul, and brought him over to Mahanaim, which is an area out of our reach, beyond the Jordan river."

"I know where it is," I mutter.

To this day I have never visited that place, but this I know: because of its geographical location, this stronghold is protected not only by the walls around it, but also by the natural boundaries marked by the slopes of its deep, broad valley. Clearly, Mahanaim is the perfect site to serve as a sanctuary for important fugitives.

Why I neglected to consider it when I was hunted by Saul is a complete oversight on my part. Now I make a mental note to myself: if I ever become a fugitive again, this would be my first place of refuge. The mental note is followed by another: I tell myself, stop thinking like a wanted criminal. Be confident. You are a king now, are you not? What are the chances of having to run for your life?

Meanwhile Joav presses on. "Ish-Bosheth is a wimp, but he has better credentials than you. I mean, he's Saul's son, his heir."

"I know it, and I understand what you mean," say I. "In the eyes of most people, the crown should go to him, not me."

"The crown should go to the one head that can carry it."

"And the other head? What about it?"

"So far," he says, casting a sharp, examining look at me, "none of the assassins I've sent out there managed to put their hands on him."

At once I tense up.

"What?" I cry. "Did I tell you, at any time whatsoever, to send assassins? Did I even hint at such a hateful idea?"

"Your majesty." Joav bows, but only slightly. "Between you and me, there's no need for explicit instructions, is there? The last thing you want is for someone—anyone who wishes to get a cozy job in your court as a historian—to overhear such instructions and then, unwittingly, to record them. Right?"

Dumbfounded I look at him as he twists his lips into a cold, cunning grin.

"You can rely on me. I always know what's best for you," he says. "What's more, I'm always ready to act on it."

I hesitate to tell him, "That's just what I'm afraid of."

In turn he says, "This is no time to be faint of heart. Events are happening fast, and we must respond faster. Abner can gather a big army before you know it."

"I know it."

"He has set a crown on Isb-Bosheth's head, and propped him up as a king over all eleven tribes of Israel, which of course, complicates matters for you."

"It does."

He sets his hand on the hilt of his sword. "The loyalty of your own tribe, the tribe of Judah, can't be enough for you. To ensure that your house, the House of David, will last, the first thing you need is the support of the rest of the tribes."

"True," say I. "And they need mine."

To the sound of his sword clinking, Joav bows before me. "No one but you can lead the fight against the Philistines. I've seen your skill on the battlefield. Without it, our very existence is in question."

"But," say I, "as long as they have a descendant of Saul as their king, the other tribes won't come around to see reason, nor will they offer their support to me."

"Unless," he says, passing his finger fondly along the blade, "they suffer a major defeat."

"Joav, they're our brethren," say I. "I don't want to spill blood, theirs and ours."

At that, he laughs. "Ha! What's wrong with bloodletting? Waging a little war every once in a while is a time-honored tradition. And what's more, it's such a fun game! I take great pleasure in it."

"Unlike me," say I.

To which he bares his teeth in a smile.

"There are times," he says, "when we must tell our conscience to shut up, especially when it interferes with our having a good time."

"Enough of that," I scowl at him. "We have been trying to establish the borders of our territory, which is a hellish task, given to daily setbacks. Faced with strife from within and without, I know one thing: what we need is a convincing triumph over the Philistines."

"Which only you can achieve, your majesty."

"With such a victory, our brethren will eventually come to kneel down before me. So I'm certain I can bring this unnecessary, senseless civil war between us to an end."

"No," he says. "That you can't do."

"Why not?"

"Because," he says, with a drawn-out, patient tone, as if explaining a grownup concept to a slow-witted child, "it hasn't even come close to a real beginning."

*

Over the next few days I keep turning the situation in my mind, weighing the prospects of different ways to reach out to the elders of Israel, or even to their leader, the newly anointed puppet king, Ish-Bosheth himself, because I think I understand him. The crown may weigh him down. He may wish to get out of a shaky, precarious position as a figurehead propped up by the real power behind him, his first in command, Abner son of Ner.

But before I can decide on my best move, word comes to me that they have already made theirs. It may not look significant to you—but to me it is. Abner son of Ner, together with Ish-Bosheth son of Saul and his men, left Mahanaim and went to a highly symbolic place in our history: Gibeon.

This city is in the territory of their tribe, the tribe of Benjamin, but it holds great fascination to the entire nation. Why, you ask? Because according to ancient lore, this is the place where God made the sun stand still during our battle with the Amorites.

So in choosing to go there, Abner calls not only for the support of his tribe—but for the attention of the entire nation: all twelve tribes, including my own.

This move is a direct affront to me, to my rule. It suggests that the Lord will surely grant them victory, even make the sun stand still to expose our military weakness, and to aid them in spilling our blood, because according to them, He is on their side.

I can just remember how Michal daughter of Saul, my first wife, would cast doubts on the will of an invisible deity. I imagine her hugging the bronze icon of the Baal, leaning it on a pillow of goat's hair for its support, then turning her eyes to me as if to ask, Well? How can He be on the side of every side in every battle?

And I would say, God knows!

At this new turn of events, bringing peace about is an even more crucial task. On one hand, this task cannot be entrusted to anyone else but me. On the other I must start delegating some of my responsibilities, because such is the way to to achieve efficiency in the complex business of ruling. I try to reason with myself that after all, Joav is my right hand man, the sharpest, most capable commander in my service.

In reply I ask myself, can I trust him to open peace talks with the other side? Will he obey my orders? Am I his master, or does he entertain the notion that—quite to the contrary—he is mine?

I am a king, I tell myself. Truly, I am!

Perhaps Ish-Bosheth son of Saul is whispering to himself the very same words.

There is an odd symmetry between him and me, as if a strange mirror reflects all aspects of his reality into mine. In the wake of his father's death I have ascended to reign over the tribe of Judah, and he —over the tribes of Israel. Now, both of us are trying to cope with a political muddle, which makes it difficult for both of us to find our bearings.

The similarities do not end there: Like me, he has to contend with a strong military leader, one who offers support and at the same time, is gradually becoming a threat.

My Joav is his Abner.

I am a king, Ish-Bosheth may tell himself. Truly, I am!

Perhaps he, too, is afraid to hear his first in command ask him, Really? Are you?

And so, in spite of my better judgement, I send Joav on a diplomatic mission, to meet his Benjamite counterpart, Abner son of Ner, at the pool at Gibeon. This is one of the most strikingly beautiful sites in our land. I imagine that it would be the perfect backdrop for the two of them to shake hands.

Yet for some reason I have a suspicion, a nagging suspicion that with a few choice words, these equally cruel, equally ambitious military leaders may opt to move things in the wrong direction, and plunge us all into a blood bath.

Joav mounts his horse and rides out of the compound. At the bend of the road I spot his two brothers, Abishai and Asahel, waiting for him to lead the way. I listen to the sound of the hooves, and only when it dies out do I notice the pounding, the heavy pounding of my heart.

Perhaps this is an ill-conceived mission, one I may regret in the days to come. Even so I am learning my role, and my best teachers are my mistakes.

Let the Boys Play Before Us

Chapter 2

Few places have an air of mystery as much as the pool of Gibeon. When you gaze upon this monumental, rock-cut architecture, it inspires you to think of the possibility of man ensconcing himself, in perfect harmony, in the womb of nature.

Constructed by the giants who inhabited this land a long time ago, a massive wall encircles the crown of the hill. In the immense rock just inside it, they excavated a huge pool, with a spiral staircase of steps, seventy nine large steps cut into the stone walls, continuing downwards into a tunnel that provides access to a water chamber, deep below the level of the city. This is where I wish to find myself, perhaps with the one woman I cannot have, because for me this pool is so remote as to be a complete retreat from the world.

It should take no longer than a couple of hours to reach this place on foot from Hebron. Peering out from my window at the empty courtyard below I watch the shadow as it crawls, ever so sluggishly, from one mark to the next one around the sundial.

The hours swell into a day, and the day drains into night, during which the shadow dissolves. Meanwhile, the rhythm of time slows down, it becomes immeasurable—until, at long last, the sun peeks over the mountains and starts a slow, strenuous climb along its heavenly arc, which is when the shadow is reborn.

Growing shorter as morning turns to noon, and longer as noon turns to evening, it moves around the sundial at barely perceptible degrees, until pointing due east. Then it fades, together with the sunlight.

Darkness rolls in. Night falls. And still, no word from Joav.

By now I have climbed up and down the stairs several times. I find myself pacing nervously to and fro, in and out of the gate, then round and round the courtyard.

I am irate, and quite angry with myself for being such an inexperienced king, and for allowing myself to be left in the dark.

Why, why did I neglect to send along someone fleet-footed, someone who can run faster than anyone else in my army, and bring me a reliable, timely report of what is happening there, in Gibeon? Joav's youngest brother Asahel comes to mind.

Slender and quick, and at times too impulsive for his own good, he is the only one I truly like of the three sons of my sister, Zeruriah. I like the name she gave him, too. It means, made by God. There is something striking about his beauty, it is so precious that looking at him you cannot forget, the way you do looking at other people, that he is God's creation.

Why didn't I talk to him before sending my men out?

I become focused, singularly focused with the need to talk to Asahel. It takes hold of me to such a degree that by daybreak—when the sound of marching rattles the walls, and my first in command, Joav, comes in, finally—I neglect to ask him about his mission, except to blurt out, "Where is he?"

The general strikes his familiar pose, holding his hands tucked behind him. I am glad not to look at them, because often, when Joav comes in after a military skirmish, they are bloody all the way up to the elbows. "He, who?"

"Asahel."

At hearing the name Joav grinds his teeth, a furious, terrible grind that makes everyone else step away from him, which at once brings me to my senses.

Now I notice the wild, unusually ferocious look in his eyes.

He groans, "Am I my brother's keeper?"

"Aren't you?"

"Enough!" Joav snaps. "Don't talk to me!"

I have never seen him this way. Joav is known to keep his cool even in the midst of the bloodiest of battles, which is why I have come to rely so heavily on him. But now his face is darkened, and his jaws—tightly clenched.

In place of an answer, a strange sound rolls in the back of his throat. Unable to control himself any longer, he wipes his bloodshot eyes and turns away from me.

I turn to his brother, Abishai, and demand of him, "What is it? What happened there, in Gibeon?"

And he says, "Nothing for you to worry about, your majesty. We come to you with news of victory."

"Peace," say I, "would have been better."

He reports, "Nineteen of our men were found missing. But we've killed three hundred and sixty Benjamites who were with Abner."

"Don't expect a medal for it," I grumble.

"Peace," he mumbles, "is not going to happen."

"Then," I tell him in a dry tone, "what you bring me is not what I intended. It's a disastrous win."

Abishai hangs his head low between his shoulders, as if it were a burden. Perhaps he is searching for an answer.

So I ask him, "What is it? You're holding back something else. I can tell. With such a magnificent, decisive victory, as you seem to think of it, why is your brother, Joav, behaving like that?"

"Because," says Abishai, in a choked voice, "such is his way to grieve."

"Grieve?" I peer into his eyes. "Over what? Never before did I know Joav to show emotions."

"Neither did I."

"Well? Tell me what happened, already."

"Asahel," he whispers, "is dead."

*

During the time I served as a captain in Saul's army, fighting the Philistines, and then as a servant of the Philistines, fighting against the Amalekites and other peoples, I have seen my share of young soldiers, dying. Without a doubt, this experience has hardened my heart. Which is why I am stunned, I am utterly surprised to discover the extent of my sadness over this loss.

What an agile boy he was! What an eager, curious look glinted in his eyes, and what an angelic, innocent face! His death touches me in a new way, which I cannot immediately put into words.

I spend the remainder of the day with my men, many of whom are wandering about with a shocked, traumatic expression. Such is the face of victory.

I try to ease their pain by telling them how grateful I am for their sacrifice. The only one I avoid is Joav. I keep a distance from him because in his grief he seems wild, and more dangerous than ever.

After sunset I go up to my chamber, unfurl a scroll of papyrus and sit there, staring at it. My reflection in the darkened window casts back a vacant look. The quill trembles in my hand, and the papyrus shines in a peculiar way, which makes it seem more blank than ever, with the moonlight glancing off the edge. The task of recording, even for myself, what I have learned about the incredible events of the last two days, that task is quite daunting to me.

Yet this I know: recording what happened is crucial. It is something I cannot trust to any old historian—even if he belongs to me—because writing is my way of going through this loss, and through regret.

What a disastrous triumph! Describing it is one thing. Understanding my failure to prevent it is quite another.

Exhausted I close my eyes, only to force them open again. The voices of my men rise to me from the courtyard below.

Their stories start melding into an image of that place, which brings to me, quite vividly, how it happened: how a questionable victory was claimed, at the cost of young lives destroyed on both sides.

I dip my quill in the inkwell and bring it to me, hovering over the papyrus in wait for the first letter.

Even in the faint, flickering light, you could spot the rocks at the bottom of the pool. Floating over it, reflections of the damp wall, the stairs carved into it, and the armed figures crouching upon them rippled across the glassy surface.

If you listened closely you could detect a thin trickle somewhere in the back of the cavernous chamber. Drip, drip, drip, came the pinging of water. It slipped over the edges, fingered the cracks, and dipped into the stony depressions, as if to try, to smooth the rough surfaces, and soothe the anxiety in these hard, troubled men with a breath of hope, a whisper of the possible coming of peace.

My men and the men of Ish-Bosheth clutched their weapons nervously. My first in command, Joav son of Zeruiah, sat still for a long while. At the opposite end of the pool, so did Abner son of Ner. Everyone knew these two generals are spoiling for a fight. More precisely, they are eager to watch others fight.

Then Abner stood up.

He raised his voice, to make sure that it would carry across the length of the pool. "Joav!" he called.

And Joav called back, "Here I am!"

And Abner said, "Let's have some of the boys get up and play before us."

"Play?" said Joav.

"Play?" sang the echo, bouncing all over between one craggy slab and another. "Play... Play..."

"You know perfectly well what I mean," said Abner.

And the echo chanted, "Mean... Mean..."

"All the same," said Joav, "let me hear it."

So Abner spelled it out, he said, "Let your boys and mine fight hand to hand here, in front of us."

"All right, let them do it," said Joav.

The young men stood up, and one by one they were selected by the older ones and sent to the middle, where Joav and his army on one side and Abner and his army on the other could all enjoy the spectacle. Twelve boys for the tribe of Benjamin and Ish-Bosheth son of Saul, and twelve for the tribe of Judea and David were counted off to play their last game.
Then, to the cruel sound of cheers, clapping, and cussing, each one grabbed his opponent by the head and thrust his dagger into his side, and together, slicing and convulsing, they fell down.
And the surface of the water, which had been so clear up to now, became dark. Red streams started swirling, spreading in it. Life seeped out of their bodies as they laid still over the lip of the pool, which was now utterly muddied with blood.

I read what came out of my quill, knowing that so far I have not even started to touch upon the worst part.

When I had slain Goliath, both sides had taken the result to mean one thing: the battle had been decided. So the Philistines had escaped. We had pursued. But here, this was a standoff. How do you call the battle? Both sides won. Both lost.

This was no longer a minor military exercise. To decide the winner in this game, it would have to turn into something quite different: the beginning of war.

Fighting that day was fierce, both armies flying at each other, daggers drawn. By the end of the day, Abner and his men were defeated by mine.

Now, difficult as this may be for me, I must take a deep breath and tell you what happened to the youngest of the sons of my sister Zeruriah.

Now Asahel was as fleet-footed as a wild gazelle. He chased Abner, turning neither to the right nor to the left as he pursued him.
Abner glanced behind him and asked, "Is that you, Asahel?"
"It is," he answered.

And Abner said to him, "Turn aside to the right or to the left; take on one of the young men and strip him of his weapons."
But Asahel would not stop chasing him, neglecting to consider the experience of the older man.
Again Abner warned Asahel, "Stop chasing me! Why should I strike you down? How could I look your brother Joav in the face?"
But Asahel refused to give up the pursuit.
So Abner thrust the butt of his spear into Asahel's stomach, and the spear came out through his back. He fell there and died on the spot.
It was such a horrific sight to behold that every man stopped when he came to the place where Asahel had fallen and died.
But his brothers, Joav and Abishai, continued to pursue Abner, and as the sun was setting, they came to the hill of Ammah. Then the men of Benjamin rallied behind Abner. They formed themselves into a group and took their stand on top of a hill.
Abner called out to Joav, "Must the sword devour forever?"
And the echo rolled across the landscape. "Forever. Forever. Forever."
The echo had spoken, but Joav remained silent, which reduced Abner to pleading for the lives of his tired troops. Facing death made him see reason, all of a sudden—or else, he calculated that the art of war is to gain time when your strength is inferior.
"Enough," he said. "Don't you realize that this will end in bitterness? How long? How long before you order your men to stop pursuing us? Are we not brethren?"
In spite of the rage in him, Joav found himself forced to answer, "As surely as God lives, if you hadn't spoken, the men would've continued pursuing them until morning."
And he blew the trumpet, and all the troops came to a halt.
All that night Abner and his men marched through the prairies, deeper and deeper into safety.
They crossed the Jordan river, continued through the morning hours and returned to their base in Mahanaim.

*

I rinse the tip of my quill with water from the jug. At this point I can no longer go on writing.

I am utterly spent. Even so, one thing is clear to me: I must find the words for one more thought, a thought that is too nebulous, too vague to describe, which is why it keeps coming back, again and again, to trouble me.

It has to do with Joav. Who knows what pain, what shame he conceals in his heart over his brother's death. He is a danger to himself, and perhaps to me too.

I have not spoken to him yet, nor would he talk to me this entire day. Even so, his actions speak for him. While I was eagerly awaiting his return from the pool at Gibeon, he took a strange, roundabout path to come back.

Instead of bringing the body of his brother back here, into our compound—or else, calling me to come out, to join the funeral procession, so that I may preside over it, even give a memorable eulogy for all to weep over the fallen—Joav chose to do something quite different.

Accompanied by my entire army, he took Asahel and brought him into his father's tomb in my home city, Bethlehem. He interred him there, before marching all night and arriving here, at Hebron, by daybreak.

Do you find his roundabout journey—up and down the land, from Gibeon to Ammah to Bethlehem and then, back here—a bit strange? I do. It makes me wonder why Joav decided to exclude me from this particular military funeral, even though he knew that his brother was so dear to me.

Perhaps this is his way to tell me that I cannot share in his grief, that it is private—but with multitudes of soldiers standing still around the crypt, this makes little sense.

So I figure, this must be his way to tell everyone that it is his war now—not mine. This is about vengeance. To him, the corpse of the enemy always smells sweet.

Which makes him unpredictable, and more dangerous than ever, particularly because he has such a brilliant military mind. If he continues to make my moves for me, this land has no chance for peace.

I must find a way to control him, or—failing that—to neutralize his growing power, because he is a menace not only to my opponents, but also to me.

Time to Act

Chapter 3

Starting a new job is never easy, least of all this job, where I am constantly being compared to my predecessor—only to end up falling short. I am challenged in all respects, all but one: my people say I am a man after God's own heart.

What that means, God knows.

Centered in a provincial city, the city of Hebron, my reign is limited to the territory of my own tribe. Even so, ruling is not as easy as I hoped it would be. I have known it all along, have I not, that Saul's mantel would lay heavy upon my shoulders. But youth has a way of shrugging off any threat, any notion of failure.

Perhaps I should not have reached for his crown. But sensing his weakness, how could I resist?

But enough about him. This is about me, and about how I am learning, step by step, to climb a rocky landscape. I have lived through my share of scandals on my way up, which sets a challenge before the historians, those who used to work for Saul. They will have to prove themselves to me, by finding a way to shed a favorable light upon my previous stunts, or else drenching them in obscurity.

From now on things will be different. I wish to find redemption. I dream—with a strong drive, a conviction that may exceed my capabilities—to chart a course in history for my tribe, and perhaps for the entire nation.

Of one thing I am sure: I may stumble, I may make my own mistakes—but never will I repeat his.

To this end I study every one of his actions, as recorded in the few scrolls that have been recovered, now that his dismembered head is finally resting in peace.

My adviser, Nathan, knocks softly at the door and takes a hesitant step into my office.

In place of a reply I shake my head, hoping to be left alone. For more emphasis I step out to the balcony overlooking the view.

There is the Road of the Patriarchs. It follows the watershed ridge line of the Samarian and Judaean mountains, running from Megiddo and Hazor south to Beersheba, skirting around our compound. The road is utterly deserted, no one in sight.

For a minute I have a vision of how it might look in the future, when peace is finally here, and merchants start coming. They start bringing exotic goods from faraway places to an increasingly rich population, with no fear of being robbed. The vision brings the sound of hustle and bustle throbbing in the air, as a long caravan of wagons comes into view and out again, leaving behind whirls of dust.

For now, there is only silence.

"Look out," I whisper, mostly to myself. "A tortuous road lies ahead. There is not one place, not one angle from where you can see each and every bend. How can you prepare yourself? How can you guess what's coming at you?"

"Your majesty?" says Nathan. He talks sheepishly—but looks like a goat.

"Not now, leave me alone! Can't you see I'm having an important conversation?"

"With yourself?"

"Even so," I say, keeping my gaze away from him. Alas, his fine, wispy beard is such an unpleasant sight, to both of us.

I imagine him clasping his hands together and praying to the Lord every evening, asking to be endowed with a full, flowing beard with fluffy curls, the likes of which prophet Samuel used to have. Nathan would do anything to have it.

He even wears the same sack, made out of the same rough cloth, for no better reason than to remind people that he, too, has that look, that aura of authority, and thus should be considered a man with divine wisdom.

Nathan clears his throat, trying to call attention to his presence. Despite his meager appearance—or maybe because of it—he is starting to gain fame as a spiritual being, one who talks with the Lord.

I wait for him to cough again and then, "You again," I grumble. "What is it this time? I'm busy learning to become a king worthy of the crown, and meanwhile there you are, opposite me, trying to become a man worthy of the cloth."

"If you need me," he offers, "here I am."

"Not now," I mutter, knowing that with him around me I must guard myself from my weaknesses. The last thing I wish for is him telling me the moral of my own story.

I lean over the railing, wishing to be wrapped, somehow, in the warm evening breeze. It comes and goes, stroking my face one minute, and the next one, trembling upon it.

"The wind goes toward the south," I murmur to myself, "and turns around to the north. The wind whirls about continually, and comes again on its circuit."

"Your majesty?"

"That which has been is what will be," I say dejectedly, thinking that this idea is so old, that it lacks any hint of originality. There is no point of writing these words, let alone publishing them. In the future, any fool can claim them as his.

"Your majesty?"

"That which is done is what will be done, and there is nothing new under the sun."

"I'm at your service," says Nathan. "How can I help?"

At last I relent, and turn to him.

"You tell me," I say. "Studying the history of Saul—"

"God bless his soul—"

"Yes," say I, a bit irate at him daring to interrupt me. But then, before I can complete my sentence, I see a vision of my predecessor floating, somehow, over the landscape.

Down there where he is buried, under his old tamarisk tree, perhaps Saul can hear roots spreading through his broken cranium, and petals rustling, swaying up there in the breeze, opening overhead to a divine desert light. Perhaps he can taste salt rolling off the leaves with every drop of morning dew, washing away the blood on his pale, cracked lips. Perhaps, cradled there in the earth, he can finally find what he always wanted, and what I, too, am praying for.

Redemption.

"God bless his soul," I whisper, "and have pity on all of us."

"Amen," says Nathan, in his pious tone.

"But now, Saul is there, and here I am. So you tell me: in your opinion, what's the gravest mistake he made?"

"That's easy. Falling on his sword."

"And," I say mockingly, following the crooked line of his logic, "allowing those Philistines to fasten his head to the wall of the city of Beth Shaan, that wasn't such a smart move either, was it."

"That," he agrees, "was the last, most inevitable misstep in a journey that had been troubled all along."

"But back at the beginning," I say, "back when he was still learning the job, what was his most fundamental error in judgement, back then?"

Unsure what to say Nathan twiddles the feathery end of his beard between his fingers.

"This," I state, "is what I think: to his misfortune Saul came to rely on one, and only one adviser. Old prophet Samuel."

"So?" says Nathan, a bit indignantly. "I see nothing wrong with that."

"Don't you?" I glower at him. "Given such dependence, how could the king hope to survive the struggle, the political conflict between him and one opposite him, the man of God?"

Before he can figure out what to say, the office door swings open and my second advisor, Abiathar, comes in.

He has great credentials, being the son of the high priest at Nob, and the fourth in descent from our legendary priest Eli. Like Nathan, he is considered to be a holy man. They constantly argue with each other, so that to my delight they balance each other out.

My third advisor comes in behind him. Ahitophel the Gilonite has been in my employ for only a short while, which may explain why I am having a hard time figuring him out.

What I dislike about him is his mood swings. When his advice is not followed, his eyes darken and he starts moaning and groaning profusely, which is why I rarely ask for it.

Even so, I mean, even without my invitation, Ahitophel offers his opinion. It is known to be as sound as that of one who inquires of God, which means he is invariably more perceptive than those who listen to him.

I don't want to listen to him.

On his way to join us on the balcony Ahitophel passes a quick glance around the office. "Your majesty," he says. "Where's your first in command?"

"Joav? He's doing what he enjoys most," say I, pointing at the smokey blue outline of the hills down there, outside the city, far beyond the walls. "Practicing military maneuvers, in preparation for a raid."

To which Ahitophel says, "May I speak freely? I know no other way to offer my advice to you, but to be utterly honest."

"Why, I wouldn't have it any other way," say I.

And he says, "If you don't like what I'm about to say, I would gladly go home." In a lower voice he sighs, and I am unsure if he is truly depressed, or just likes to make noises to draw attention to himself.

"Hell," he sighs again. "I would go there right now and hang myself."

Nathan and Abiathar exchange glances, after which I suggest, "No need for such morbid thoughts, Ahitophel. Just say what's on your mind. And no need to take your life over something as minor as rejection, is there?"

He says nothing in return, so just to offer myself as an example I tell him, "When I was in Saul's court, he hated my music with such passion as to wish me dead. Talk about rejection! Time and again I would dodge his spear, hoping for nothing else than to stay light on my feet, to save my life. Every escape was a thrill, every moment was like being born anew."

"Birth," he says, gloomily, "was the death of me."

To which Abiathar clucks his tongue, and Nathan cackles under his breath.

"Enough, both of you," I command. "And you too, Ahitophel. Do I need to ask again? What's on your mind?"

And he says, "First, let me observe one thing: what you're doing with us is quite clever. Granted, advice is a nice thing to consider from time to time, but you let each one of your political and religious counselors understand, all too well, that he is merely one of many. This way you may keep yourself out of mischief, and above the fray."

I lean into his ear. "I hate to be that transparent," I whisper.

"You are," he whispers back, in a confidential manner. "But only to me." And aloud he suggests, "You should extend the same approach to your military advisors."

"What military advisors? I only have one."

"Exactly," says he. "You have come to rely on one, and only one general: your nephew, Joav. If he decides to challenge you, what then? What would you do?"

I shrug. "I've been thinking of this problem, to which I can find no solution. I mean, what choice do I have?"

"You could lead the army myself, like Saul used to do."

"Given my latest distaste for engaging in battle, I'm glad that Joav does it for me. He bloodies his hands, so mine can remain clean."

"Clean hands," he counters, "do not absolve you from responsibility."

"Even so," I insist, "I must rely on him."

"What you must," he says, "is this: create a military hierarchy. Two generals reporting to you would be a more stable support than a single one."

And when I say nothing Ahitophel flashes a winning smile at me. "You know I'm right, don't you," he asks, not expecting an answer. "At this point, we have the upper hand in this ill-advised civil war against the eleven tribes of Israel and their so-called king, Ish-Bosheth son of Saul. His general, Abner son of Ner, knows all too well that he is on the losing side. How about relieving him of his misery, and reaching out to him?"

This question, I must admit, is better than any advice. It brings to mind what I already know, but forgot to consider: there is trouble brewing between those Benjamites. Abner has been strengthening his own position in the house of Saul, so much so, that he has now made a bold move against his master.

Of all things, it has to do with a woman.

Her name is Rizpah. Everyone knows that even though Saul is no longer among the living, his concubine remains off limits to other men, because making love to her means you are doing the unspeakable: taking possession of that which belongs to the king.

It may seem a bit convoluted to you—but trust me: around here where I stand, the logic is utterly clear. By getting into the sack with her, you tell the public that you are stepping into his shoes, and thus, vying for his crown.

This is a bold move for the general to make, because it exposes Saul's son to ridicule as a weak heir to his father's throne.

Heaven forbid I should ever get stuck at either end of such an awkward, sticky situation. I aim to be careful, and never bring wrath upon myself by touching another man's wife. More importantly I hope no one ever touches mine.

Just thinking about such possibilities makes me shudder. With a shaky hand I reach up for my crown and straighten it on my head.

I hope it is safe.

Nathan shakes his head in disbelief. "Did Ish-Bosheth ever find out about the two of them?"

"Did he ever!" I say. "My spies tell me that he went to his general and asked him, 'Why did you sleep with my father's concubine?'"

"Oh Lord! What a public disgrace!"

Over his interruption I say, "Perhaps so, but knowing his own power Abner was furious, not because he had to explain the sordid affair, but because in his mind, no explanation was needed, really, when talking to his own sock puppet—even if it wore a crown."

Nathan raises his head to heaven as if to say, Oh Lord! There is only one power! And say what you will, this is such a shame!

I press on with what I know is going to be a long-winded story—but not before taking a deep breath, so it may last me to the end of it. "The general raised his voice, he shouted, 'How dare you ask me that? Am I a dog's head? To this day I've been loyal to the house of your father Saul and to his family, but it's a big stretch being loyal to you. Give thanks, you spineless wimp, that so far I haven't handed you over to David! Yet now you accuse me—me!—the man to whom you owe not only the misshapen crown on your head, but having a head in the first place! Don't you get it? You owe me your life! Oh hell, what's the matter with you? You think you are king? What a laugh! You think you can charge me with an offense involving that woman? Think again! May God deal with me—be it ever so severely—if I don't do for David what the Lord promised him, and transfer the kingdom from your hands, from the house of Saul, and establish David's throne over Israel and Judah all over the land, north to south, from Dan to Beersheba!'"

Nathan is too dumbfounded to chant, "Oh Lord," so he just stands there, clasping his hands together as if ready to pray, and staring at me.

"After that," I say, with a throat that by now starts to feel scratchy, "after that, the puppet king didn't dare open his mouth, let alone say another word to his first in command, because by now he was afraid to lose his life, such as it is."

"Now that," says Nathan, "is a cautionary tale if I ever heard one."

To which I say, "True. I pray I would never end up in that place. For me, to live defeated and inglorious, and under constant threat from my own man, is to die daily."

"Think about what you've just said," Ahitophel tell me. "Your Joav is just like his Abner."

"Don't I know it."

"Now," he stresses, "is the time to act."

And I say, "What d'you suggest I do?"

And he says, "The moment is ripe for change. Abner is angry, which means one thing: he may consider a bold move, bolder than taking that woman to bed."

"Which is what?"

"He may leave his master, and defect to our side."

"Really?"

"Really," says Ahitophel. "And if he does, you may divide military power between him and Joav. I urge you," he says, "talk to him. Time is dear."

Nathan and Abiathar are speechless. They must be mulling over the story. The silence between us remains unbroken, as evening descends.

Ahitophel leans on the railing and casts an eye down there, at the view. It is truly magical.

Dabbed with darkness, the rooftops below us seem to have fallen into disarray. Some of them slant this way, others that way, and some, at the bottom of the untidy heap, lay utterly flat. Their edges are sharp here, blurred there, and from one moment to another, uncertainty grows.

On the flat rooftop directly below my tower there is a large puddle from last night's rain. Now it reflects a first glint of moonlight. Captured in reverse in the depth of that surface, the stars seem to be falling instead of rising in the night sky.

In some corner down there, sheltered under a shadow, stands an unused, dust-covered bath tub, which I hope no one else but me has spotted. For me it marks a trace, a fading illusion of a woman in the nude, just starting to raise her eyes to me.

"Now," says Ahitophel, "is the time to act."

Another Man's Wife

Chapter 4

As a poet I play with flowery expressions. As a politician I arm myself with them to achieve my goals. The more difficult it is to overcome my opponent in the war of words—the more I enjoy sharpening my weapons.

All morning I have been recounting the reasons why Abner, the general of the other side in this uncivil war, should defect to our side. I have been turning words around, deleting and adding phrases, to suggest an idea that at first—without the power of expression—may seem absurd: his treason towards his puppet king, Ish-Bosheth son of Saul, would be cast by my court historians into a winning combination of wit and courage.

But before I can seal the note and send it to Abner, his messenger arrives at my door, with an urgent plea. Which tells me one thing: the general is far more desperate than I have suspected.

My victory is at hand. This time it is coming with barely any effort. Alas, it is all too easy. What a letdown!

The Benjamite messenger bows before me, while removing his hat with a fancy, flamboyant move. I note that it is not too dusty, and neither are his shoes, which means that he has come here, to my compound in Hebron, from a nearby place. Perhaps his master, Abner, is waiting there for him, eager to get word of how I would react to what he has to offer.

"Well?" I say, in my most commanding voice. "Speak quickly, will you? I don't have all day."

And the messenger—a young fellow chosen, perhaps, because of his flair for acting—strikes a pose, the overly confident pose of a general with his hands tucked behind his back so as to thrust his breast forward, and his chin held so high as to risk falling backwards.

"I speak for a great commander, famous for his unparalleled military mind, a fighter who is a worthy opponent, and an even worthier ally," he says, in a splendid, grandiose tone.

To which I say, tersely, "Cut it short."

"He—not his king, Ish-Bosheth son of Saul—is the one who holds real sway over the eleven tribes of Israel, who are fighting against you." The messenger claps a hand, ever so theatrically, to his heart. "I speak for my esteemed master, Abner son of Ner. He sent me here to ask you this: whose land is it?"

"That," I say, in a firm voice, "is a question that needs not be asked at all. This is, without a doubt, my land! It belongs to me and to my rule alone, and to no one else's. Your master knows it."

Which confuses the messenger. Shifting uneasily from one foot to another he gulps air once or twice and waves his hands about, flailing to find the words, just the right words for his prepared speech. They escape him for the moment. To baffle him even more I turn my back on him and start walking away.

"Here's my advice to your master," I say, casting my voice at him over my shoulder. "You mustn't fight too often with me, or you'll teach me your art of war, which is why your side is suffering heavy losses."

"Wait!" cries the messenger.

But I keep my pace, and increase my distance.

So he runs after me, throws himself at my feet, and catches his breath long enough to say, "I beg you, wait! My master says, 'Make an agreement with me, and I will help bring all of the tribes of Israel over to you.'"

"Ah!" I exclaim. "Now you're talking!"

Then I control myself. Why should I betray any sign of excitement? No one should suspect how badly I need Abner.

I must have him on my side, so I can divide military power between him and my own first in command, Joav, whose ambition is starting to manifest itself. I must cross one sword with another, so not one of them will threaten me. Only then will my throne be stable.

So I say, with coolness in my voice, "With or without his support, I shall prevail against your master. Abner knows it, and so does anyone watching this war. The tribes of Israel will join my own tribe, the tribe of Judah, with or without him. It's just a matter of time."

For lack of a comeback, the messenger stutters, "But, but... Are you prepared to wait?"

"Is *he*?" I counter.

His face is contorted with bewilderment. By now the messenger must have realized that his script is faulty, because it is lacking enough prepared arguments for a chance to win this discussion.

I tell him, "Time is dear—and so is blood."

Then, to help him out of his misery I add, "All the same, coming to an agreement with your master is an interesting idea—but it has its price."

He holds his breath, so I press on. "Tell your master: I demand one thing of you. Do not come into my presence unless you bring my wife, Michal daughter of Saul, when you come to see me."

*

Despite having five wives around me—or perhaps because of it—I have been thinking lately about her, even pronouncing her name, and listening to my own murmur.

Michal.

Somewhere in my heart I have a soft spot for the princess who saved my life, even though she turned around soon afterwards and did the unthinkable: she married another man, while still being my wife. You may ask, can she do this? Really? By law, is it even allowed? I thought it was not—but then, consider this: she is the daughter of a king and can do as she pleases.

For her, being connected to a wanted criminal, a traitor with a lousy reputation such as myself, must have been distasteful. It was something she decided to avoid at all costs, even if it meant falling into the arms of the first suitor that came along.

How desperate must a woman be for such a hasty move!

Then again, any marriage is, inherently, a hasty proposition. I mean, if you think about it long enough you will never do it. It is easy to succumb to a moment of temptation—but nearly impossible to stretch it out, and prolong it for the rest of your life. Alas, lust cannot last.

Except, perhaps, if you long for your beloved, but cannot find her again, except in your dreams. Her absence, then, becomes a constant companion to you.

But I digress. I do not want to think about Bathsheba. Instead, let me think about my first wife.

I remember Saul's daughter the way I saw her that last time: bending out of her bedroom window, fastening the end of a long piece of fabric to some hook right there, below the windowsill, and lowering me down the tower by it, knot by knot, so I might escape her father's assassins.

How strange, almost beautiful she was, her hair slinking out of the jeweled coronet and blowing in wild gusts of wind, and her face flashing out of the darkness as bolts of lightning crackled in the air, shooting down into the garden below us.

At the last second, just before I let go of my end, her face dimmed out into the shadow above me. I was facing death, and I knew it, but somehow I found the courage to whisper, "Will you kiss me?"

I thought I spotted a sparkle in her eyes, or perhaps it just seemed that way. Perhaps all I saw was a mere reflection of torches, streaking through the paths of the garden below my feet, their flames flickering in the air, shining brighter as the soldiers came, drawing dangerously closer.

"No, David," said the princess. "Not now."

And flying down, I cried, "When, then?"

Her answer could barely be heard, because of a clap of thunder, but I thought she answered, "When you deserve it."

This I know: being eager to please me, Abner will pull the strings on my behalf. He will threaten his puppet king, Ish-Bosheth son of Saul, so the order will come out his mouth to take Michal out of her husband's arms and send her, with a military escort, back into mine.

Clearly, there is a plausible legal justification for this maneuver, because everyone knows that I betrothed her to myself for the price of a hundred Philistine foreskins, and everyone remembers that just to be on the safe side, I paid her father, Saul, double that price.

Any other king would demand that you kill a dragon to win his daughter's hand in marriage. Not so Saul. In accordance with his strange demand to me, two hundred Philistines had to part with their private member, and flesh had to be ripped apart, just so I could have her. I was forced into being an over-achiever.

So now there is no doubt, is there, that she belongs to me.

*

A week later, by a royal decree issued by Ish-Bosheth, Michal is taken by Abner away from her new home, the home of the man she married when I was away. His name is Paltiel son of Laish. He must have been living in constant fear ever since the wedding night, knowing that one day I would reach for his beloved and snatch her, one way or another, away from him.

He goes with her, weeping behind her in public in the most miserable way, wailing and moaning and howling like those two hundred Philistines put together, as if his manhood was on the line.

I suspect that the princess kept him away from her bed all these months, and told him—with the same proud tone that still rings in my own ears—that he does not deserve her.

I guess, nobody does.

Paltiel goes on making a fool of himself all the way to a place called Bahurim, which is where the road takes a sharp turn into the Jordan valley, close to Mount of Olives.

Then Abner says to him, "Enough already. Go back home!"

The poor loser turns tail. At long last, he goes back.

At hearing about this I shake my head in astonishment. Oh Lord, whatever calamities await me out there in the future, let me never come to that same turn of the road! Let me never lose all control of my destiny, and become the subject of ridicule, all because of another man's wife.

Perhaps the princess expects to see me immediately upon her arrival, but I take my time. When she knew me I was a nobody. Now I am king. Let her wait.

Back then Michal was a riddle to me, because she was my first wife, and because I was immature. Now I find that experience is overrated, because to my surprise she seems more mysterious now than ever before. I mean, while her dear husband was whimpering, and wiping his eyes and his runny nose, and moping about behind her, what was she doing?

"What was she doing?" I ask the general, Abner son of Ner.

"Not much," he says, removing his helmet and scratching his head. "She seemed to be in a daze."

And I say, "Really? What, not a single word, not a single gesture? No hug for that blubbering fool of hers, or a kiss goodbye, or any other hint, minute as can be, of affection?"

"None of that." He shrugs. "And who cares?"

"I do!"

A thick clay bottle with a delicate, long neck is set on the table between us. I swig the wine, then slide the thing over to him, thinking all the while that with him, as with most people, I must avoid using the poetic style of my thoughts and instead, speak plainly.

The general clasps it between his large paws, empties it in a single gulp, and throws it into the corner, where it breaks to smithereens.

"What's done is done," he says. "That's all there is to it."

Now that Michal is back, which means that he has accomplished what I asked of him, here we are: two fighters meeting in secret, to negotiate important matters, matters that are more serious than what's in a woman's mind.

For example, the possibility of peace.

I suggest one idea after another, all around the same topic of how he might assist me in bringing his tribe, the tribe of Benjamin, and the other tribes of Israel to join my tribe, the tribe of Judah. Once a nation rises out of of these fragments, the war between us will be a thing of the past. At long last, all of them will accept me as their king.

The general listens and nods his head from time to time, down here in my private cellar, in the back of my compound, away from the watchful eye of my own first in command, Joav.

One thing is clear: Joav, whose skill with knives is unmatched, cares nothing about peace. He abhors it, because he thrives on shedding blood.

And he is not likely to stomach my idea, I mean, the idea of dividing military power between him and his Benjamite counterpart. He would not surrender to it, not only because for him it is a demotion—but because of a bitter family feud. He is bent on avenging the death of his young brother, Asahel, who was murdered by Abner just a few weeks ago at the pool of Gibeon.

Of this I am certain: if I fail to control him, Joav would find a way, sooner or later, to exact his revenge.

And so it is best to wait for the right moment, and take every precaution, before I announce—to him and to my entire army—the rearranged military hierarchy. For now, the only one to know of this meeting is my trusty soldier, Uriah. I send him to fetch a few more bottles for us.

Meanwhile the general, Abner, leans across the table to me. He is a broad-shouldered man, and the wooden surface creaks under his weight. He wipes his tired, red eyes. They must feel scratchy to him because of the dust of the road.

For lack of something to say he bares his teeth in a smile. "To peace!"

To which I smile back. "To peace!"

Then I rephrase my earlier question, but both of us know that it is still the same. "Tell me," I ask, "was Michal crying or smiling, during the journey?"

"Her mouth was pursed into a straight little line. I couldn't tell."

"Was her face utterly blank? Was it devoid of expression for an entire day?"

"Of what importance is it, what a woman does, what she thinks," he mutters. "And anyway, such was her upbringing, right? A princess, especially one who grew up in the court of a madman, learns to keep a stiff upper lip."

"Even so!" say I. "Really, I don't understand her."

"Your majesty." Abner drums his fingers on top of the wooden planks. "I can't figure her out any better than you can."

"Could you detect any sadness in her—not just for him, but for herself as well? Was Michal brooding, perhaps, lamenting her fate, the fate of a woman used as a pawn in a political struggle, which is instigated by men?"

"Such," he says, simply, "is a woman's role."

"But," say I, "she is a king's daughter."

"Which means she's a trophy, an expensive one." He spits on the floor. "Why would she brood over it?"

I give him an irate look, so he goes on to ask, "What's the matter? She belongs to you, right?"

It is then that I have to admit, "This is a question I ask myself quite often, because—just between us—here is a little secret: I think of Michal as another man's wife."

He chuckles.

"What's so funny?" I ask.

And Abner says, "That's exactly what her husband told me."

"Really!" I exclaim. "How strange!"

Meanwhile, Uriah comes into the room and sets a couple of bottles in the middle of the table. Then he retreats, ever so humbly, back into the shadows. Being a foreigner in our land he is mindful of his accent, and prefers standing in the rear of the room, ready to serve, without saying a word, so Abner and I can ignore his presence.

Having uncorked one of the bottles, the general takes a sniff of the wine, and relaxes into his seat.

So I decide that this is the best time to test him, and test my own thinking, too, on a more personal note.

So I say, "I hear you're having an affair with Saul's concubine, Ritzpah."

"Yes," Abner says, with an acid tone, which he intends to wash away with a drink. "And what a delight that is."

"So, just like me," I say, as if to confide in him, "you must have discovered one thing: taking a woman that belongs to another is a temptation unto itself."

"I assure you, it's more trouble than it's worth," he says, already uncorking the next bottle.

"Really?" I ask. "It is?"

"Because of her I must now leave a steady position with my master, and defect to you. Oh trust me, I appreciate the opportunity, I do! But an affair with another man's wife? I would never do that again—unless, of course, it's a way to gain something else, such as political power."

I go on to ask, "So, if she were a regular wife, I mean, the wife of a regular soldier, and could offer no political gain—none whatsoever—would you start an affair with her?"

"No," he says, firmly, and again he spits. "Never."

"Not even if you were in love?"

"Love?" he echoes, as if this were some foreign, Babylonian word, written in hieroglyphs onto a brittle papyrus scroll, by our neighbors south of the border, the Egyptians, and read out with a twist, in the heavy, indecipherable accent of our neighbors north of the border, the Hittites.

Abner may be right. For a simple word, it packs a complex emotion.

"Yes," I say. "Love."

He claps his hand on the table, and the empty bottles start bouncing about. "Hell, what does that have to do with anything?"

His Abner is My Joav

Chapter 5

I should have been more careful setting up this meeting, and I know it—but this time, in spite of my better judgement, I allow myself to be bold. Listening to what I have just said, I realize that *allowing myself to be bold* may imply that I am in control of my actions, which is utterly wrong. They are driven purely by impulse at the moment.

I am overtaken by glee, because of two things: getting word from the Benjamite commander, Abner, that at long last peace between our tribes is close at hand, and sensing that with it, my crowning moment —and I mean that literally—is soon to follow.

So when he comes back to the compound, this time with twenty of his men, and all of them snap to attention at my sight, and hail me as the next king of the land, I make the mistake of throwing a huge public feast. I bring in my men as well—all of them, except my first in command Joav and his soldiers, who are busy, as usual, raiding some poor villages somewhere on the other side of the Jordan river.

At my command, the doors of the largest hall in the compound are unlocked. Their hinges are rubbed with oil, so there will be no creaking sounds, no annoyances. This is the perfect place for celebration, which is why we never used it up to now, for lack of reason to do so.

I tell everyone to come in and mingle, never mind if they belong to the tribe of Judah or the tribe of Benjamin. We are true brethren now, as we were always meant to be. We are family. We are of the same blood.

Newly acquired, sumptuous rugs are spread across the stone floor. Wall sconces are set aflame, so the place glows with color and warmth. Large pillows, embroidered with silk threads, are brought in, so we can all recline upon them, and relax into a sense of luxury. Lavish food is served. Wine starts splashing into cups.

I trust, perhaps foolishly, that generous hospitality removes the divisions between us, and ushers in a new era.

And so, with great flair, I raise my cup to toast my former enemy, Abner. "Shout with joy to the Lord!" I cry out.

He shouts.

Over his bellowing, I pray, "Let them be ashamed and confounded, those who seek after my soul. Let them be turned backward, and put to confusion, those who desire my hurt."

"I'm yours now," he says simply, clinking his cup with mine. "And what you've just said, that describes the man I used to serve, Ish-Bosheth son of Saul. It's time to put him to shame and confusion."

"And," say I, "to relieve him of his crown."

Everyone repeats my words. "Relieve him we shall!"

"Lets start over," I urge them. "Lets move upward and onward, from conflict to concord!"

On a whim Abner pours his cup over his head, and red wine squirts all over him. I cannot help but imagine him forging ahead in the heat of battle.

"The days of fighting are numbered," he declares. "No more civil war!"

"*Civil* war?" I repeat, finding myself having to correct him. "Let's not call it that. There was nothing civil about it."

By now both of us are drunk, but in my case it is not because of alcohol. For me, it is an overwhelming sense of euphoria. Peace is almost here. Bloodshed is about to become a thing of the past. Let our wounds heal.

Enumerating the names of the tribes and their territories, "Gilead is mine," I announce, with exaggerated confidence.

And he concurs, "So it is!"

So I add, "Manasseh is mine! Ephraim also is the strength of mine head! Judah is my lawgiver!"

"So they are, so they are! The land is yours, it's practically in your hands!"

Then I call out the names of our mutual enemies, because at this moment there is nothing better to unite my guests, and the entire kingdom, than a common sense of threat. We have been bleeding too long. Under my rule, we can start scrubbing together at the grime of years.

"Moab," I says, "is my wash-pot! Over Edom will I cast out my shoe! Over Philistia will I triumph!"

Everyone cheers. "So you will, so you will!"

One cries, "To peace!"

And from across the room, another one counters, "To victory!"

Finally I ask Abner to speak up, because all of us should hear the good news he is bringing.

Sprawled upon his pillow, "Listen, y'all! Hear me out!" he exclaims.

To which my men yelp. "Hush now! Let the Benjamite talk!"

And he states, now with a slightly slurred speech, "I conferred with the elders of all the tribes of Israel, and—quiet there, pay attention now!—I said to them, 'For quite a while you've wanted to make David your king. The time is now, do it!'"

"Really?" one wonders out loud. "They've wanted to crown our David?"

"No," says another. "But somehow, saying so makes it true, even in their own minds."

Meanwhile Abner presses on. "I didn't stop there," he says. "I told the elders, 'Don't you know? The Lord promised, *By my servant David I shall rescue my people Israel from the hand of the Philistines and from the hand of all their enemies.*'"

I look at him with surprise, unable to decide if he has become religious all of a sudden, or just manipulative.

Has Abner ever heard the Lord, let alone obeyed Him? I have my doubts. Has he intended to strike the fear of God in the hearts of those stubborn elders, so they bend to his will, and act on his suggestion?

Abner winks at me. He raises a hand, to stop his soldiers and mine from interrupting him again until he is ready for it.

"After that," he says, "I also visited the territory of Benjamin, and spoke to their people in person, because more than any other tribe, their loyalty has been—until now—to the house of Saul."

"So it was." They nod their heads. "Until now!"

Abner rises heavily to his feet, and once he finds his balance up there he bows down before me.

"Your majesty, let me go at once," he says. "I'll assemble all Israel for my lord the king, so that they may make a covenant with you, and that you may rule over all that your heart desires."

To which I say, "Go in peace."

And having leapt to my feet I reach out to him and shake his hand, making him my equal, so everyone can see the trust between us. There is no need anymore for shields and arms.

Then we dispense with formalities altogether, and embrace each other in parting.

Abner gathers his soldiers, and out they go. The doors clang to a close behind them.

Little do I know that this is the last time we meet.

In my elation I run up the stairs, all the way up to my office, and I go out to the balcony to watch the long evening shadows of their horses fly across the hilly landscape. They gallop away. In a blink all I can see in the failing light is dust, puffs of dust kicked into the air by their hooves.

The sun starts dimming behind the horizon. It's the end of the day.

"Here's for a new beginning!" I call out to him across the growing distance, and I hope the breeze carries a whisper of my good wishes to him.

*

"What the hell have you done," a voice cries out, with an alarmingly sharp tone.

I turn around to face an unpleasant surprise. The man I feared would find out about the feast I threw this evening, my first in command, is coming out after me, eyes blazing.

For now I disregard the foul language, which no one in my court but Joav allows himself to use in my presence. Others may think he uses it because of familiarity, as he is my nephew, the son of my older sister Zeruriah—but I know better. He would like to believe that I rely exclusively on him for my military expeditions, and I think, not for much longer.

Right now, with my back to the railing, I must do what I can to bring him to a halt. So without as much as a glance at the rooftops below us, I glare back at him, as hard as I can, so he may keep his unspoken hate in check.

"Damn you!" he growls at me.

"Stand back," say I, in my most commanding voice, because I am always mindful of the knives hidden in the folds of his clothes.

He obeys me, quite unwillingly, and takes an unhurried step back, which for me marks a strange slowing of time. The air between us seems to sizzle, spattering one fleck after another. And in a blink, the faces of my wives start flickering in my mind. What will their fate be, I wonder, if anything happens to me?

Their images glimmer one after the other. Here, here is my first bride, Michal, whom I have not even seen since her return to me. Perhaps this is why she comes to mind the way she looked back then, on our wedding night.

I remember: Her skirt slipped, it cascaded down from the waist, revealing another skirt underneath, and another one under that. Lace over silk over some starched fabric, each layer gave out a different sound, a different rustle as they collapsed onto the floor, creating one ripple around another around her.

With her narrow hips and her flat belly, which was matched by an equally flat chest, she looked so much like a boy. And trapped in that skinny body, pounding there with palpable longing, I could sense the heart of a woman, a proud woman, cursed with love.

The silvery moonlight outlining her image dims out, and she vanishes—only to be replaced by another woman, the one who visits me in my sleep. What a vision of beauty she is, which makes me ask myself, what will happen to my dreams when I am gone? Will they fizz out, too?

Alas, no one ever comes back from that other side to give us any answers, do they? So I wonder, when the body dies, is the soul immortal? What will last, when I am swallowed by the void? Who will be left to imagine her, rising from the foam?

In profile, her lashes hang over her cheek, and the shadow flutters. Bathsheba brings her hand to her lips and ever so gently, blows off a soap bubble. It comes off the palm of her hand, then swirls around in the evening breeze, becoming more iridescent until its glassy membrane thins out.

Even as it bursts, and nothing is left but thin air, I keep glaring at Joav.

"What have you done?" he groans, clutching his sweaty head with both hands, as if to freeze a throbbing pain.

To gain time I answer with a question, "What's the matter, Joav?"

He counters, angrily, "What d'you mean, *what's the matter*? Here I go, risking life and limb on the frontline—"

I match his fury with my coolness. "You're leading your men to those uncalled-for raids at your own pleasure, not mine."

"I do it to bring you not only glory but plunder, too—only to find out that which you hide from me—

"Which is what?"

"You think I don't know?" he cries.

To which I say, "Know what?"

He starts pacing back and forth, from one end of the balcony to the other, as if putting siege to a city. "Ha! You think I don't hear things, even if I'm not here in person?"

"I have no secrets from you," I say, brazenly. "Perhaps I should have."

He seethes at me. "Behind my back, you've been bold enough to entertain the worst of my enemies, the one who has the blood of my brother, Asahel, on his hands."

I move away from the railing, leaving him standing there, alone. "You've been in the business of war long enough to know better. One can't hold a grudge forever."

"You're quite wrong about that," he says, with a note of bitterness. "I can."

"Then, stop it. Vengeance clutters the mind."

"Wrong, again. It sharpens it."

"There are casualties on either side," I argue, "some of which may be unintended."

He stammers. "How, how dare you say that to me?"

I cross him on my way back into my office.

"Careful now," I warn him from in here. "Don't you raise your voice in my presence."

Joav plucks nervously at his mustache. Then he follows me, making an effort to lower his voice. "You weren't there, were you?" he hisses at me. "You didn't bear witness how 'unintentionally' my brother was slain."

"It was my mistake, sending you on that mission, in the first place," I must admit. "Had I been there, that silly game you played with the lives of their boys and ours would never have been played. And as for your brother—"

"What about Asahel?" His voice reaches a new high. "Are you accusing me for his death?"

"I'm accusing no one," I assure him. "Not a thing is to blame but this sorry state of war."

"I'm not my brother's keeper!"

"Who says you are?"

"It wasn't my hand that thrust the butt of a spear straight through his stomach, till it came out through his back, was it? Every man stopped when he came to the place where Asahel had fallen, where he died. Not one of them moved—except me."

"A horrific sight it must have been."

"I can still see him lying there, convulsing in a puddle of blood, mouth open as if to call my name."

I take a step forward, wishing to embrace him, to try and relieve some of his sorrow, but then the thought of the knife hidden somewhere behind his back stops me from reaching out.

"What a grisly sight," he says, groaning. "Damn it, it's burnt into me, into my eyes, even as I try to shut them. I carry it, it comes after me, chasing me like a curse, wherever I turn."

"Then let it go," say I, "or walk away from it."

"Never."

"Let us make peace with our brethren."

"Ha! You must be kidding me."

I plead, "Come to peace, Joav, with yourself most of all."

"Don't you lecture me!" he cries, in a tortured tone. "Words, words, words! I have no interest in them."

"Joav, you speak like a madman."

"My actions," he says, with a tone of warning, "will speak for me."

"I can imagine you," say I, "hunting the killer. I can imagine him, running away."

His eyes narrow to a slit as he asks, "Can you?"

I do not wish to describe the scene to him, because I was not there to witness it. But I paint Abner in my mind, his face reflected from that dark, red puddle. Down there lies his weapon, having pierced its victim. He is empty handed now, and in a flash he's gone, to save his life.

"Joav," I implore him, "even if you can't forget it, I beg you now: it's time to forgive."

"It's time," he says, "to cut his throat."

"Abner," say I, "isn't here."

"What?" he mutters, in surprise. "You let him go?"

"Listen to me," I stress. "We have a chance to end this feud."

To which he says, "What do I care."

"Well, as my general, you should," say I. "Why? because I say so. I rely on Abner to bring the elders of the other tribes to their senses. With his help they will fall to their knees before me."

"Ha! He'll do no such thing."

"Abner is mine, he has sworn loyalty to all of us."

"He has sworn loyalty to his own master before you, did he not?" asks Joav, not waiting for an answer. "So it's a cheap sentiment either way."

To which I say, "Even so, I must give him the chance to prove himself to me."

And he says, "What the hell are you saying?"

"Don't you raise your hand upon him."

"Ha! You can't ask that of me."

"I'm not asking, Joav." I peer into his steel-grey eyes. "I'm ordering you."

"What a laugh!" he says, with a last-ditch effort to provoke me. "You think you're the king."

I grit my teeth and, ever so calmly, I counter, "I do, and I am."

Exasperated, he bangs the palm of his hand at my desk. "Don't you see what you've done?"

So I try to explain, "I've done what's necessary for my plan, for unity in this land."

Joav shakes his head, utterly in disgust.

"Look, Abner came to you. It was such a rare opportunity! Why, why did you let him go?" he asks, not wanting to hear me. "Now he's gone! You know him. He came here to deceive you, to observe your movements and find out everything you're doing."

"I'm prepared to take that risk."

Joav is grinding his teeth with an ear-piercing noise, which rolls over his words, so none can be discerned. So I press on.

"His actions," I say, "will speak for him."

"By then," he grumbles, at last, "it may be too late."

"Late for what?"

"For me to catch up to him."

With that he turns away, and as abruptly as he has come Joav leaves the office, his knives clinking against each other in a secret compartment, somewhere under his belt.

He slams the door on his way out. I hear the thump of his footsteps shaking the stairs, one at a time, all the way down to the ground floor. I should send someone to lay a hand on him and bring him to a stop —but I know few will take that risk.

I find myself having to contend with a strong military leader, one who may be ready, in days to come, to lead a rebellion, and force his master off the throne. Ironically, so does my counterpart, the Benjamite king Ish-Bosheth son of Saul.

His Abner is my Joav.

I can just hear the voices of these two commanders as they rise against our authority. It is hard to tell them apart. Each one of them screams, Am I a dog's head? To this day I've been loyal to you, but it's too much of an effort supporting a loser! Give thanks, you spineless wimp, that so far I haven't handed you over to the other side!

You Don't Deserve Me

Chapter 6

Tomorrow, Joav may justify his plan—reckless as it may be—as his way to obey my orders, even if no such orders left my lips. I regret not having a historian by my side at all times, to record everything I have said, and attest to my commitment to end this war. I must appoint someone to the job. More importantly, I must figure out a way to stop my first in command from chasing Abner, because if his actions are to speak for him, the injury may be fatal.

Night drags on.

The singing of lullabies down there, in the women's quarters, becomes softer and softer still. The voices of my children quiet down, and so do the voices of their mothers, except for an occasional outburst, here and there, of bickering between them.

Night drags on.

I sit at my desk, shuffle plans of fortification of the compound this way and that, mark a trail here, a street there on a map of Hebron, unfurl roll after roll of papyrus, and sharpen the tip of one feather, then another. Then, rising up, I look outside. The sky curves over me. It seems round, like a huge tambourine, and the darkness—tense enough to drum a beat upon it.

I lie down on my bed, eyes wide open. I stare at shadows, and listen to the pounding of my heart.

Night drags on.

Soft breathing fills the air, as my kids have all fallen asleep. One of them cries in his dream. It is a sudden, shrill sound, full of fear. Then he falls silent again. Again, soft breathing fills the air.

Now my wives start chatting with renewed energy. I hear them exchanging beauty tips between them. They are talking about the girls who have moved here, next to the compound, and about me. Usually I would be curious to learn what they are saying. Not so now.

Night drags on.

There is only one voice which—strangely enough—I cannot detect: that of Michal, daughter of Saul, who is my first wife, and the first Jewish princess I met, the first one anyone ever met, because we had no princesses before her in our entire history.

On a whim I rise from the bed, and run down the stairs, excited to think that at long last I will lay eyes on her again. I have no doubt that despite being brought here by force, the princess is expecting me eagerly.

Before sweeping her off her feet I will let her know that as her husband—one worthy of his crown—I plan to act magnanimously. For her sake, and for the sake of domestic harmony, I will pretend not to mind her follies all that much, I mean, her getting married, ever so conveniently, to another man while I was unfairly branded a traitor, and had to keep running to save my life.

I fling open the door, and catch my dear wives in different stages of undress. Colorful garments slip from their waists, as fabric belts are loosened and knots are untied. Scarves are crumpling into a heap, meeting their radiant reflections down there, on the polished floor. Veils are finding their rest on top of the ornamented panels that divide the space. Half nude, the women reach up to unbraid their hair.

Passing in between Ahinoam, Eglah, Abigail, Maacha, Haggit, and Abital, I promise each and every one of them in turn to get back to her, soon.

"Wait!" says Ahinoam, trying to match her step with mine.

I stop long enough to give her a little peck on the forehead. "How beautiful you are, my darling," I say.

To which she smiles sweetly, and answers in kind, "How handsome you are, my beloved!"

"Oh, how charming!" says Eglah, catching my hand and bringing it over her cheek, by which I do not mean the one on her face.

And Maacha tells her, "Leave him alone! My beloved is mine and I am his."

And I say, "You are mine and so is she." But in her ear I whisper, "Like a lily among thorns is my darling among young women."

"What?" says Abigail, from behind one of the panels. "Who are you calling thorns?"

In place of an answer I say, "Show me your face, dear, let me hear your voice."

And Abigail says, "Why? Haven't you heard me, just now?"

What choice do I have but to say, "Your voice is sweet, and your face is lovely."

"Enough with the complements already, come to bed," she says.

And I promise, "Soon."

Meanwhile, Michal is nowhere to be seen—until I step out of the women's quarters, and into the veranda overlooking the courtyard. There she stands, next to the pillar at the far end of it: a tall, skinny figure, utterly motionless, one arm wrapping the other as if to guard herself from contact.

"There you are," I say, opening my arms to her with a grand gesture, hoping that she will listen to her heart and run into them.

But no, Michal stands her ground.

With a spring in my step I dash towards her—only to be stopped by her stern look.

"This is not where I should be, and you know it," she says. "What made you abduct me?"

"Abduct?" I shrug. "What d'you mean, *abduct*? I'm your husband, am I not? Who can deny it?"

"I can," she counters. "When you became a fugitive, only a few years ago, your rights were revoked. My father made sure of it."

"That may have held true during his reign. No one dares to repeat his nasty, baseless accusations, or call me a criminal any longer. Wake up to the present, Michal!"

There is a flash in her eyes, and it gives off a heat, an unmistaken attraction, which she hides by covering her face with the palms of her hands.

Into them, "I hate you," she says. Her voice is muffled, yet the emotion rings in it, loud and clear. "I wish I could just close my eyes and never open them, and never see you again."

I reach for her, noticing that her palms are a touch clammy, which reveals to me how aroused she must be.

I recall how, on our wedding night, Michal was drawn to me, and could not resist combing through my curls with her fingers. I remember her wondering, out loud, "What is it that devastates me so? What, in the names of all gods, is this curse? What makes me want a commoner like you?"

So now, "Look at me," I say, stepping closer. "No longer a fugitive, I am the king of the land now, in place of your father, Saul."

She turns her head away.

I reach up for her chin, and turn it gently with my finger, making her face me. In a moment I will part her lips with a kiss.

"Michal," I say. "I'm not a wanted man any longer. Make me feel like a man, wanted."

Shaking her head, she admits, "I wouldn't know how to do that."

"Like it or not," I say, "I have every right in the world to take you, if so I wish."

Have her knees just buckled? Perhaps I have imagined it.

She leans against the wooden pillar, and hugs it for support. I wonder, does she play hard to get? Would she wish to be gathered into my arms in spite of her own resistance?

"Go away," she whispers.

I take her by the shoulders and draw her to me, allowing her a brief moment to refuse—but when she does not, I wrap my arms around her waist, pulling her as close as I can. And I murmur, "I'll never let you go."

"That's just what I'm afraid of." The princess bows her head, surrendering, perhaps, to a moment of weakness. "You've made me your prisoner, and I think I know why."

"That's too harsh a word," I say, waving my hand to dismiss what she has said.

All the while I know that as ugly as it may be, *prisoner* is truly the right term.

"Let me free," she pleads.

"Why, my court is becoming world famous for its fineries," say I, pointing vaguely around me, at the darkness. "I promise, you would enjoy it here."

"As elegant as it may be, this is jail," she insists. "You wish to keep an eye on me, and on each and every one of the descendants of the house of Saul, all of whom you intend to capture."

"Nonsense," say I. "I've done what anyone would expect of me."

"Which is what, exactly?"

"I've rescued you from that so-called man of yours, the one you chose to marry while still being mine."

"And who told you I needed rescuing?" she asks. For some reason tears well up in her eyes. "I was doing just fine where I was, thank you very much!"

"I don't believe you," say I.

"Who cares," she counters.

"If you were doing so splendidly great," say I, "then why didn't you hug that fine husband of yours, or kiss him goodbye before you parted ways?"

She shrugs, for lack of an answer.

So I press on. "I bet you never let him touch you. I bet you kept yourself for me, even if you'll never admit it."

She says nothing, which makes me regret allowing this unexpected anger to rise in me, and intrude between us. For a minute I consider telling her how sorry I am, but then find myself unable to do it.

Instead I remind myself to act magnanimously, which is the best way to impress a princess.

"Look, Michal," I say, in my most patient tone. "You could have remained loyal to me."

"I am," she says, "my father's daughter."

"Even so. But I forgive you."

"What?" she says, gasping. "Did I hear correctly? *You* forgive *me*?"

"Of course," say I. "I understand trying to survive, to find security. Being the wife of a traitor wasn't a good role for you, so you found your solution. I get it, I do."

"Do you?"

"Michal." I put my arm around her. "Let bygones be bygones."

And before she can think of a comeback I press my body against her bosom, pinning her to the wooden pillar. Next to my chest I sense the pounding of her heart. Slowly, tenderly, I brush my lips against hers, taking in her fragrance. To my surprise I find a trace of sweet perfume under her earlobe. For just an instant I think I catch a sparkle in her eyes.

Then she pushes me away and steps out of my embrace. With a defiant gesture she does the only thing she can do to take control of both of us.

Looking straight at me, she brings her hand to her mouth, and with intention, she wipes off my kiss.

I admire her for it.

"Don't you touch me again," says the princess.

I bow before her.

She bows back, mockingly.

"I missed you, Michal," I tell her. "I thought that perhaps you missed me too."

"You were such a fine, delicate boy when I first noticed you in my father's court. And oh, you had such charm about you. Since then," she says, pointedly now, "you've learned to use it."

"Have I?" I take a small step forward. "Then kiss me, Michal."

She takes a big step back. "Other women may swoon at your sight, because nowadays you wear a crown. That's what moves them."

"But does it fit me, Michal?"

"I must admit, the costume does look convincing on you. These jewels up there, on your head, sparkle quite brilliantly. The textiles you've chosen are in great taste, and so is the fine leather of your boots."

"What can I say? I have a fine taste, as befits a king."

"Even so I won't yield to you, because there's nothing regal about who you are, and because nothing, nothing at all has changed between us."

Which is when, at last, I bring myself to say, "I'm so sorry. Please, Michal, forgive me."

Holding her head high, she gathers her skirts about her.

"You've never deserved me," says the princess. "And you still don't."

She stand there, opposite me, for a long while, and a sense of heaviness sets in between us, which reminds me of one thing. Night has been dragging on, dragging on. And it still does.

I turn away from Michal, close my eyes, and listen. I have been laughing playfully with her, trying to amuse myself, acting as if I were carefree—but at this point, no longer can I ignore the hammering of my heart, and the pain, the sharpening pain down here, in my gut. What shall I call it? Perhaps, regret.

In place of dancing around her—for no better reason than carrying on an idle chat—I should have mounted my horse. I should have caught up to my first in command, Joav, and stopped him from chasing Abner. I should have done something. Perhaps I still can. I pray that by now, it is not too late.

A sudden swoosh of air blows through the veranda, which makes the fallen leaves hiss. They turn over and over, fizzling underfoot. I hear them get crushed, with a crisp crackle, as Michal walks away from me, holding her head high.

*

Meanwhile I pick up a new sound. Here come the footfalls of a runner. He darts across the shadows of the columns, passing her on his way, and falls to his knees before me.

"What is it?" I demand.

Out of breath, "Your majesty, don't punish me," he begs, "for what I bring you."

I raise him to his shaky feet. "At this time of night I expect nothing but bad news," I tell him.

"The news," he says, still trembling, "is worse than anything you might have expected."

"Look, I'm bracing myself for the worst. I'm ready. Tell me what happened."

"A crime."

The hammering stops as my heart skips a beat. By pure intuition I guess, "Murder?"

"Yes, your majesty," says the messenger. "A vicious, bloody murder. Everyone knows how much you rely on your first in command. He's above the law, so perhaps I should say nothing."

"Go ahead, tell me."

"To get close to his victim, Joav called him into his arms, as if to tell him some juicy, dirty joke, as old fighters often do when they get together. And then—then, while holding Abner in a tight embrace—he found that soft spot, right under the rib, and in a flash pulled out a knife, and struck him dead."

Is That the Way He Should Die?

Chapter 7

This morning, a rowdy crowd gathers outside my tower, hurling stones at the walls and threats at me, and demanding that I come out to face my accusers. By their hostility, and by their growing numbers, I know that my worst fear has come true. I am in deep trouble with my own people. A crime has been committed in my name last night, and contrary to popular belief it enrages me, too—but would they believe me? God knows! How do I convince them that I had no part in it?

Now that is going to be quite a challenge, especially when coupled with the next question: if they do not trust me, how will I manage to persuade others—such as the elders of the other eleven tribes—to overcome their suspicions?

How, then, do I respond to the murder of Abner, the man stabbed by the sword of my first in command, Joav? What do I tell my people about the particularly vile way it was committed? And even though I did not spill his blood, should I wash my hands of the whole thing? Should I shrug off any responsibility?

This day is going to test me—test what I am made of—in a way that no battle has ever done before.

I step out into the sunshine, guarded by a handful of my most loyal soldiers, who are attempting to advance in front of me under protection of helmets and shields.

Even so I doubt we can make any headway.

At first I aim for the large wooden stage across from us, at the other end of the courtyard—but to my dismay I realize that we cannot make it as far as that. Why? Because of all that pushing and shoving, not to mention the stuff that comes out of a multitude of mouths, I mean, the foul language and the equally repulsive odors.

I come to a stop right here in the center, with my back to the sun dial. Pressed upon by the rabble I see a swarm of hairy fists, thrown up in the air in my direction. Perhaps I look as if I am about to faint, which makes someone run back to my court, drag out a chair and bring it over, that I may sit upon it.

Instead I take a deep breath, and hop onto the cushioned seat. Its softness, its puffiness, and the sleek texture of its fabric, these are the things that make it unstable. Such is the curse of luxury.

I stand up—a bit precariously—on top of the thing, and raise my arms over the riffraff, the way I always do at the beginning of my speeches. It helps me find my balance.

A moment of hush comes over everyone, which I am quick to use to my advantage. I start talking.

"People of Hebron," I address them, and at once, the resonance and melody of my voice seems to fascinate those who stand here, close to me. They must find it soothing, no matter what words, what arguments I use. "These are trying times," I say, "for all of us! What better opportunity can there be to stand together, and rely on each other?"

"Yes," says one. "Together we'll stand, we'll follow you everywhere!"

And another says, "Well, it depends. What about the rumors—"

And a third says, "What about the blood on your hands—"

Over the interruptions, "You and I are one," I tell them. "We have a bond between us. All of us men, we are sons of the same tribe. The same blood runs in our veins."

Meanwhile, a shrill voice cries from a close-by roof, "And what about us girls?"

This must be the new maid hired recently by my trusty soldier, Uriah, to serve his wife. He is known to dote on Bathsheba.

I raise my eyes to try and spot her, which is not easy because where I stand, the sun is directly in my eyes.

"Come join us down here! The more the merrier!" I call out.

I hear nothing but giggles, so I follow that up with, "I am one with you too, and with men and women everywhere!"

Squinting, all I can see is the outline of my tower, and the roofs soaring overhead, a wing here, a wing there. Earlier this morning, looking down at the shadow cast by the steeple clear across the compound, I felt as if I dominated whoever lives down there, in the shelters below me. Now things are different. No longer am I at the top.

I fear a reversal of my fortune, because at this point even this maid is looking down at me. I imagine that from her vantage point I look small, nothing more than a scalp upon which she may spit, at whim.

I must bring my voice to a boom to impress them.

"I and my kingdom," I declare, with great conviction, "are forever innocent before the Lord concerning the blood of Abner son of Ner. May his blood fall on the head of Joav and on his whole family!"

I still have the magic in me. Women cheer. Men are in an uproar.

For now I decide to refrain from telling them the exact details of the murder. It imparts a bad taste, a sense of betrayal, which may irritate them. They do not need to learn that my general sent messengers after Abner, and in my name—yet without my knowledge—he lured him back here, to Hebron. Upon his arrival Joav took him aside into an inner chamber, as if to confide with him in private. And there, to avenge the blood of his brother Asahel, he stabbed his victim in the stomach.

And so, in his arms, Abner died.

I can imagine the scene but do not wish to describe it, and anyway, what good will it do?

In place of upsetting these people I must gain control over their mood. So with a dramatic gesture I take hold of my expensive mantle, and tear it apart with a single, abrupt rip.

All eyes are on me.

"Tear your clothes," I bellow, stunning them with a show of grief.

And when they do nothing but stand there, I order them, "Put on sackcloth!"

And while they obey me and start rending their garments I give a subtle hint to my guards. They leave me, and go into that chamber, and bring out the body upon a long bier. There lays Abner, covered with a white shroud.

Its wrinkles flow, they twist along with his pose, as if to sculpt the last throws of pain. Under one of the folds I catch a glimpse of his hand. There are his fingers, clutching the wound.

Some of the people may have seen it already. Others may have heard rumors about the way Abner was stabbed. No matter. I smooth the folds, so as to hide the blood from sight.

"Come," I call out. "Let us all walk in mourning, and bring our great friend, Abner son of Ner, to his final resting place."

The women know their part. They gather into a chorus, and start shedding tears and uttering an assortment of sobs.

And so, to the sound of sighs, whimpers, and occasional shrieks, I orchestrate the funeral procession. Wearing a respectful, solemn expression I walk behind the bier, and everyone follows me.

My guards whisper to me, "Where shall we go? Shall we bring him outside the city gate, and from there send him, perhaps, to his family, to the tribe of Benjamin?"

"No," say I, and on the spot I make a calculated decision to bury the body in Judea, right here in Hebron. "Let's go," I tell them, "to the heart of the city."

According to my instructions, the bier is carried to a tomb not far from the Cave of the Patriarchs, where the forefathers of our nation—Abraham, Isaac, and Jacob—are buried. This place is a reminder that we are brethren. We are the offspring of the same family.

I hope that bringing him here would become a call, symbolic call for unity to the elders of other tribes. To mourn for him in the proper, traditional way, they would have to come here, and do what Abner was working so hard, in the last days of his life, to bring about. They would have to sign a peace agreement with me.

That, in the most profound sense, was his last will. When peace comes, it will be his victory over Joav.

My heart throbs with hope. Even so I weep out loud in front of the public at his tomb. Everyone weeps with me.

Then I shake my head in a grand display of sorrow, and I chant:

"Like a fool... Is that the way Abner should die?"

One says, "No! He was a war hero. That's not a way for a fighter to die!"

And another says, "How sad for him, for all of us, really. He wasn't given a chance for a fair combat!"

Meanwhile I go on singing my lament, thinking all the while that I should have written something more elaborate, polished with stunningly intricate expressions worthy of a poet like me. I should have made sure it was ready well ahead of this ceremony. With nothing prepared—let alone rehearsed—I resort to a spontaneous performance, which forces me to come up with words as a go along:

Your hands were not bound,
Your ankles were not restrained in shackles.
You fell to your death as one felled by villains.

Listening to me, all the people weep over him all over again, which teaches me that sometimes, a rough sketch has more power in it than anything prepared in advance. Being unfinished, this lament becomes a symbol of the shrouded man's life, a life that was so brutally brought to its end.

I look around, I stir as if coming out of a trance, and ask them, "D'you not realize that a commander and a great man has fallen in Israel this day?"

"Yes," says one. "What a great loss, for all of us."

And another says, "What a great loss, for the entire nation."

And a third one come near me, and kneeling before me he urges me to eat something while it is still day.

"You're pale," he says. "We love you, and we need you to be strong, your majesty."

But I take an oath, saying, "This is a sad day. May God deal with me, be it ever so severely, if I taste bread or anything else before the sun sets!"

They take note and are gratified to hear my answer. By now I can do no wrong in their eyes. I have achieved what I wanted: word starts spreading around that I had no part in the slaying of Abner.

I am touched by their adoration, yet I know one thing: from now on I will have to walk a fine line with them. I cannot demote my first in command, Joav, for what he did. I cannot remove him from his position—not only because he is too good at what he does, but because now, with the death of his Benjamite counterpart, I have no other candidate for the job.

What choice do I have? This is the era of cruelty. The Philistines are upon us. For this nation to survive I must use the best man for the task of being ruthless.

There is no one else but Joav.

With this belief in mind, how will I convince my subjects that I am truly sorry for the crime, when I let the criminal go unpunished? How do I deflect calls to action, how do I silence pleas to do the right thing, and exercise justice?

Until now I have been careful, really careful to hide my weaknesses from view. Being a man of complexity is a private thing for me.

For public consumption I believe in a simple message: a king must seem dominant, come what may. Such is my rule, it has worked for me so far—but now, for the first time, I decide to break it.

I collapse to the ground, giving a heart-wrenching sigh, as if overcome not only by grief, but also by the long fast, which I have sworn to uphold. They gasp, and the odors coming out of their mouths make me faint all over again.

They take me back to my tower, and prop me up where I belong: on my throne.

"Today," I admit to them, "though I'm the anointed king, I find myself weak. These sons of Zeruiah are too strong for me."

"Yes," says one. "Beware of your nephew Joav."

"Beware of his brother, too," says another. "Both are dangerous."

To which I clasp my hands together, and pray out loud, "May the Lord repay the evildoer according to his evil deeds!"

Somehow, everything I say seems to please them, even this. No one thinks of asking me why, by the power of a royal decree, I would not repay the evildoer myself, instead of leaving the task to a higher force.

I am their shepherd.

They, my herd.

Assassins

Chapter 8

When Ish-Bosheth son of Saul hears that his general has been killed here, in Hebron, he loses courage. Who can blame a sock puppet for going limp in the absence of its puppeteer?

The Benjamite king spends his waking hours tearing what remains of his hair out of his head, and sighing profusely, both of which prevent him from doing much more of anything. All eleven tribes of Israel become alarmed at this extravagant display of frustration.

If I were in his shoes—which thank goodness, I am not—I would issue a call to arms. I would set out of the territory of his tribe, the tribe of Benjamin, and head directly into mine, to avenge Abner's blood. Instead, according to my spies, he doubles up on his naps. Perhaps he figures that the best cure for impotence is excessive sleep.

Two of his men—one named Baanah and the other Rekab—conclude that this is the time to get rid of him. Having had enough of his lack of action, they figure that his days are numbered, anyways, and the best thing for them would be to hurry up the flow of history, if only by a nudge. They must do it at once, because other people may betray him before they do.

What better way to do it than assassinate their king, expecting to reap the rewards from me?

So they set out for his house, planning to arrive there in the heat of the day, while Ish-Bosheth is taking his noonday rest. They go into the inner part of the house, which is where wheat is stored, and where it is given away to the hungry.

No one would ask any questions of them, there.

They need not have worried, because—due to lack of organization—the place is poorly guarded. And so, the assassins find him in his bedroom, by the snores. Having stabbed him, they cut off his head. Taking it with them, they travel all night, and arrive here, at my court, by sunrise.

"Greetings," one squeals before me.

"Blessings," squawks the other.

I take my time pacing around them, noting the blood dripping from the sack, which is held in their hands.

I can guess what it contains, simply because the sight of it brings to mind a moment from my youth, when Saul's soldiers escorted me to his court. There I stood before the king with Goliath's head cradled in my arms.

Unlike these fellows I took good care of my trophy. I hugged it with both hands, becoming one with the slain giant. Being a great entertainer I kept turning the head side to side, to study the effect it would have upon the spectators. I could see the terror, the palpable sense of superstition in Saul's eyes. By the shudder that went through his spine I knew he asked himself, what if this motion would cause Goliath, somehow, to bat an eyelid? What if he raises a bushy eyebrow? What if he drops his chin?

Saul would never have admitted his fear of me—but clearly, that was what made him propose to me, suggesting that I marry his daughter. Now these two fools may have heard about the birth of my baby girl, Tamar. Even though she is years away from adolescence, they may think I will reward them for the kill, and that I will do it in a like fashion.

But unlike me, they do not know how to put on a good show, to impress the court. What they hold in their hands could bring everyone to their knees, had they exposed it. I can just imagine the still yawning mouth, with the jaw fractured and some of the teeth chipped, because the head must have slipped.

Yes, it must have fallen off the bed and rolled about in the dirt, before they could lay their grabby hands on it.

In life Goliath must have been much more imposing than Ish-Bosheth could ever hope to become. But death has a way of bringing out the dread, no matter how immense or how shrunk the scalp may be.

Alas, what a missed opportunity! Instead of putting it on display, Rekav and Baanah wrapped the thing in a dirty old rag, which saps out not only the blood—but also the possibility for awe.

Unsure of my thoughts, the two clowns exchange glances. My silence proves too heavy for them to bear, and so is that soggy sack. Finally, shaking the tattered thing, "Here," cries one, "is the head of Ish-Bosheth son of Saul."

I glare at him, decidedly unimpressed.

Perhaps he figures I did not understand his accent, the accent of a Benjamite, when he has blurted out the name of his victim. Feeling the need to spell things out at greater length, he mumbles, "I mean, your enemy, who tried to kill you."

"He did?" say I. "Now, this is news to me! All I hear is that he is too busy following one nap with another."

"Not anymore," says the other, taking an unsteady bow before me. "This is one slumber from which he will never awaken."

"And in his dream," say I, "he must be seeing both of you. Can you feel his gaze? D'you know the words that must be coming to him?"

In confusion, he shrugs.

So I lean closer and breathe in his ear, "I can just hear his voice, saying, 'Without cause they hid their net for me. Without cause they dug a pit for my soul. Let destruction come upon them unawares. And let the net which they hid catch them. Into that very destruction let them fall.'"

I turn away, so as not to watch the way they are shaking. With slow, deliberate movements I mount my throne.

Looking down at that stained thing hanging from their fingers I tell myself, here is what I can become: a dismembered head, without the protection of that which has crowned him.

In the past, despite wanting him dead, I held my hand back from slaying Saul, because of one overriding consideration: respect for the office. I mean, he had been anointed. And so, by extension, is his son.

If I celebrate his death, if I reward his assassins, how can I hope to be obeyed by my own subjects, when the sanctity of the crown is violated? How can I hold on to power, when I am the one to have disarmed its magic?

The last words Saul said to me were a plea for forgiveness. Being a madman he could sense his fate. He could foresee my rise to power, his descent.

In my mind I can still see his outline out there, on the opposite mountain top. I can still hear his eerie voice, calling out to me across the divide, "May you be blessed, David my son. You're going to do great things in your life. You shall triumph."

Now, another one of his heirs has perished. The house of Saul is tumbling down a step further.

How the mightly have fallen.

Rekav bends his knees before me.

"Your majesty?" he says, as if to remind me of his presence.

Meanwhile Baanah forces a smile to his pale, trembling lips. "This day," he utters, "the Lord has avenged my lord the king against Saul and his offspring."

I rise to my feet, and with burning eyes I declare, "As surely as the Lord lives, who has delivered me out of every trouble, when someone told me, 'Saul is dead,' and thought he was bringing good news, I seized him and put him to death. That was the reward I gave him for his news!"

"But, but—"

Over the interruption I press on.

I bellow, "How much more—when wicked men have killed an innocent man in his own house, and on his own bed—should I not now demand his blood from your hand and rid the earth of you!"

At last, they know their fate. I intend to deter the thought of assassination, not only on my behalf—but on behalf of kings to come. I raise my hand and point at them, and without needing any hint beyond that, my men understand my will, and kill them.

To the sound of hacking behind me I leave the court, knowing that my vengeance—no, let me correct that, my justice—is being carried out to its ultimate conclusion.

My men must be cutting off the hands and feet before they hang them, for all to see. The bodies of these traitors will be on display by a pool located close by, south of the road to the sacred entrance, the entrance of the Cave of the Patriarchs.

Next to it is Abner's Tomb, in which my men will bury the dismembered head of his king, Ish-Bosheth son of Saul, with a great show of respect.

Let the puppet lay next to the hand of its puppeteer.

Bringing both of them to their final rest here, next to the bones of our legendary forefathers, will be a dual call for unity, which is so sorely needed in this battered land.

What a strange place this is turning out to be, marking not only the past, the divine promise of becoming a great nation—but also the present, the horrific strife tearing our tribes apart.

As for the future I have my doubts. Will I be able to unite our tribes into a kingdom? Will this body be made whole again?

Can we move on from the present, from this era of cruelty—or is cruelty simply the nature of the way we are, the way we are cursed to remain?

I keep walking away, away from it all, unable to stomach this brutality any longer, even as I pray for it.

You, O God, shall bring them down into the pit of destruction. Blood thirsty and deceitful men shall not live out half their days.

Having wandered about the courtyard I go back in, and enter the women's quarters, looking for something, anything to distract me from thinking, from drowning in this sudden surge of agony.

It is too early. My wives are still asleep. I do not want to awaken them, because I doubt their kisses can help me heal. I need someone to understand me—but doubt anyone can. I am lonely. My life is a constant turmoil, an unending war.

I try to imagine conquering the woman of my secret dreams, Bathsheba—but this time, for some reason, I struggle to see her clearly. Her outline is incomplete, and so is the idea of surrendering to lust.

I look up and there, under the farthest window, from which a gentle wind blows fine little puffs at the curtain, stands a crib.

I draw closer, and peek over the edge of it. Here is my baby, my precious little princess.

Tamar.

At first she gurgles, and tries to fix her eyes on me, curious to see, to separate me out of what to her must seem like a dim mess. I see myself reflected in her pupils. I see her world. It is nothing but blurry shapes.

The tiny hands flail about in the air as if to find out, by some accident of touch, who is standing above her, whispering, "Oh, little one, this seems like chaos to me, too."

I pick her up and rock her gently, back and forth, back and forth. Simply holding this tiny bundle takes a load off my heart. I brush my lips over her scalp, careful not to touch the tender spot, right here at the top. The fine fuzz of her hair tickles my nose, which brings me to a sneeze.

Then an incredible thing happens: Tamar not only looks at me—but for the first time her eyes widen, and she sees me, and wraps her tiny fingers around my thumb. Now her mouth opens into the sweetest, loveliest smile, and she coos at me in recognition.

I never experienced anything like this moment before, because I never bothered to spend time with my boys when they were this age, not even with my first born, Amnon. Stricken by happiness I feel her little heart pounding next to mine.

I close my eyes, promising myself to be the best father, and to protect her, now and in the future, from all trouble.

It is time for me, for all of us, to end this civil war. For her sake, and for all my children, it is time to give peace a chance.

The Anointing

Chapter 9

In my childhood I learned from my father that olive oil was applied to wounds to soften them, so they may heal. It was also rubbed on the leather of shields, so they may become supple and fit for use in war. Old women worked it into their wrinkles, hoping to smooth them out so their faces might regain a youthful shine.

So when old prophet Samuel visited us in Bethlehem, and took out his horn of oil, and without much of an introduction he smeared my head right there, in the midst of my brethren, it seemed a bit strange to me—and so was the expectation of everyone around me, that the Spirit of the Lord would instantly descend upon me, and stay with me from that day forward.

Perhaps that was the moment I came of age—but just exactly what that meant was quite unclear, and to this day, it still is. Life remains a bewildering thing, no matter if you are a shepherd or a king. In both cases you do your best to figure it out. And in both cases you try to find a safe place for the herd, and lead the way with a show of confidence that hides, somehow, how lost you find yourself most of the time.

I remember the smell, the unique fragrance of that oil, which stayed with me for several days after he rubbed it, with a forceful hand, into my curls.

If not for obeying my father, who told me to behave myself and stand still already, I would have taken to my heels and run back out, and never seen old Samuel again.

I tell you, that was one strange concoction! Mixed together with a dash of powdered bark and a pinch of scented medicinal leaves, it could easily mask body odor, even sweat. No wonder it had been invented in the heat of the Sinai desert, during our exodus from Egypt, and then passed down the generations, from one priest to another, that they may minister unto the Lord.

My father whispered the sacred formula in my ear:

'Take thou also unto thee the chief spices, of flowing myrrh five hundred shekels, and of sweet cinnamon half so much, even two hundred and fifty, and of sweet calamus two hundred and fifty, and of cassia five hundred, after the shekel of the sanctuary, and of olive oil... And thou shalt make it a holy anointing oil, a perfume compounded after the art of the perfumer."

I learned these words by heart, finding his singsong chant so exotic, so incredibly musical:

"And thou shalt make it an oil of holy ointment, an ointment compound after the art of the apothecary: it shall be an holy anointing oil. And thou shalt anoint the tabernacle of the congregation therewith, and the ark of the testimony... And thou shalt sanctify them, that they may be most holy: whatsoever touches them shall be holy."

Being young and ignorant I could intone these sentences, without grasping the full meaning of being anointed. Not so now.

Having waited here in the provincial city of Hebron, having idled about seven dull, long years, which seem to drag on forever, and having dreamed of a change, I know that my moment has finally arrived. I know it because of the knocks at the gate, which is where the elders of all the tribes of Israel have come, at long last, to answer my call for unity.

I am told that the oldest of the elders holds a flask of oil.

Advancing slowly through the courtyard, and into the narrow path cleared for him in between my men, a shrunken old man with leathery wrinkles leads the rest of the elders into the compound. He comes to a stand before me. Bent by years, he might as well forgo the customary bowing before me, but to my surprise he does it anyway, and nearly topples over.

Having recovered his balance he takes a labored breath.

"We," he says, "are your own flesh and blood."

"Your tribes and mine," say I, "we have been apart too long. Too many wounds have been inflicted on both sides."

"In the past," he says, "while Saul was king over us, you were the one who led Israel on their military campaigns."

"Luck," say I. "And then, glory."

To which he adds, "By the will of God."

Thinking this chitchat is leading nowhere I begin to wonder how long it will take him to go through his prepared compliments.

With fake respect he says, "The Lord said to you, 'You will shepherd my people Israel."

"How d'you know what the Lord said to me? You making it up?"

"Perhaps I am, but does it matter?"

"I guess not."

He tries a different variation on the same theme. "The Lord said, you will become our ruler.'"

"Seven years," say I. "Seven years you had to wait, till you came to this conclusion?"

"In the large scheme of things," he says, "what is seven years between us? Just enough time to puff out a breath."

"To the Lord, perhaps it is," say I. "Not to me."

The old man shrugs.

"Let us make a covenant," he says, "before Him."

I hesitate to ask, "What kind of a covenant?"

He goes on to explain, "To keep His commandments, and His testimonies, and His statutes, with all your heart, and with all your soul."

And I say, simply, "With all my heart, and all my soul, I shall."

Then I remove my crown and bow before him, so he may do his thing and rub my head with his magic potion. He tips the flask, and oil starts dripping over me. And oh, the smell! I breathe it in, intoxicated by myrrh and sweet cinnamon. In a blink, it takes me back to my childhood.

I could not have known it back then—but now I do! This ceremony marks the beginning of a new era.

What troubles it will usher in, God knows.

I see drizzles shining upon each one of my shoulders, getting absorbed, little by little, into widening stains. The garment is ruined, but who cares? I find myself utterly lost, lost in a new sense of happiness. Perhaps this is how it feels when divinity wraps over you, taking you in.

Opening my arms to the old man I dash over to embrace him. In my excitement I lift him off the ground, in spite of him shaking his head and kicking his legs and making little noises, trying to signify resistance. Perhaps he does not want to get oil stains on his own garments.

Having put him down I run around the courtyard, and with great vigor I shake hands with each and every man standing there, paying no heed to class and tribe distinctions.

I laugh, I cry, "Let Israel hope in the Lord!"

And everyone echoes, "Hope... Let us hope in the Lord..."

Raising my eyes to heaven I clap a hand to my heart. "Save us," I implore Him, "from the gulf deep here, within us."

"And," says the old man, "between us."

"Guard us," I pray, "from a smile that bares sharp teeth."

"Amen."

"Give us strength to withstand our faults, our weaknesses. Against ourselves give us a shield, a sheath."

"Amen."

My voice climbs to its fullest volume, it hovers over the courtyard, rolling over the entire crowd. "With Him there is mercy. With Him is plentiful redemption. He shall redeem us from our iniquities."

The oldest of the elders takes the crown, rises to the tips of his toes to reach up to me, and places it—ever so carefully—on my head.

And then, then the sound of trumpets bursts out.

At last, the tribes have united. A nation has been born. Israel has a newly anointed king. Me.

*

Later, when everyone has cleared the courtyard in the heat of the day, I feel an urge, an irresistible longing to talk to someone, anyone. Perhaps Michal.

For some reason, she was the only one to stay indoors when the rest of my wives came out dancing, which surprised me, because I half-expected them to complain about me getting my clothes dirty, which complicates things for doing the laundry, because nothing gets oil stains out. Instead they graced me with hugs and kisses—all except my first wife.

I find her sitting by one of the mirrors in the women's quarters. To my surprise I note that she has arranged her hair in that horribly fancy style, the one she had on our wedding night.

I remember how she looked back then, standing in her elegant chamber, in the midst of her maids, waiting for them to remove the jeweled coronet from her hair, which was gathered up in a towering bun, fancier than any hairstyle I had ever seen before. At the time it made me wonder, how would she lie down in bed with it? How would she manage to fall asleep?

I remember the long, frizzy wisp of hair that flew out of it, which she quickly tucked back. The maids rushed in and plaited it into place again. Again, she was proper.

Not so now.

Without the luxury of having a small army of servants assigned to her, she has resorted to combing her own hair, which to her must seem like an impossible mission. It must have taken her the better part of the day to gather all those hair strands, and twist them upward, and fasten them somehow together at the top of her head, hoping the bun will stay there, pointing up more or less.

The thing looks utterly ridiculous, and so do the heavy chandelier earrings dangling from her earlobes.

By her own words she hates me, and would never care to adorn herself for my sake, so why would she bring her jewelry here? That, I suppose, is anybody's guess.

Of one thing I have no doubt: at the sight of her earrings, any lesser man would have chuckled.

I chuckle.

Michal stamps her foot, casting a look at me as if to say, Don't you dare! Don't you laugh at me!

"You look lovely," I say. "Truly you do."

As a poet I trust words. Words are good for me. They are the best way to explain away my behavior. I mean, to lie. By her grimace I know that she knows it.

"Who cares," says the princess, "for the opinion of a commoner."

The scorn in her voice enrages me, and the only thing I can do to calm myself down is to recall an image, the long-forgotten image of the iron shield, which I saw in her father's court long ago, on my first visit there. I used to brush my fingers—when no one was looking—over the sharp ridges of the engraved inscription.

It said, *The House of Kish*. To a naive observer it may have seemed like an emblem of a highly respected ancestry—but as everyone around the country knew, Saul had no royal blood in his veins.

"Remember your bloodline," I suggest to her. "Your father is the son of Kish, whose nobility could be measured, with great precision, by what he owned: three donkeys. Saul came from a long line of peasants."

To which she says, "He may have been the son of a farmer—but I am the daughter of a king."

With a slight bow, "Today," I say. "I am king, just like him."

"Even so. I am the second generation of a royal family, which means one thing: I belong to a dynasty—you don't."

I hold myself back from telling her that her dynasty, such as it is, would soon become a thing of the past. That shield has no shine to it anymore.

It was left behind, half buried in dust, on the battlefield of Mount Gilboa, when in his despair Saul fell on his sword.

But even without words, what I think may be transparent to her. With a quick gesture Michal wipes the corner of her eye, so as not to allow tears to well up.

I catch her hand and bring it to my lips.

"Kiss me, Michal," I whisper.

To my amazement a blush spreads across her face. Then it deepens even more, perhaps out of shame for having blushed.

Helpless to stop it, "No," she says, proudly. "You don't deserve me."

"Didn't you hear?" I ask. "Today I've been anointed—"

"Really," she says, with deliberate coolness, looking away from me.

To which I say, "Really."

I hold myself back from telling tell her that I admire how much effort she puts into trying to annoy me.

Instead I say, "Michal darling, how incredible you are! No one can be so completely unimpressed with me."

"No one but me," she counters. "I'm unimpressed not only with you—but also with that primitive ceremony, earlier today."

"You mean, my anointment?" I say, incredulity ringing in my voice. "I don't believe it! Is that what you call primitive?"

"It's far worse than that! It's downright common. Any simpleton can do a better job at it." And in a teacherly tone, which is so typical of her, she goes on to explain, "Even hunters anoint themselves, they do it with lion's fat in order to gain courage, and to strike fear in other animals."

"Then, be my lion," say I.

She cannot help but correct me. "You mean, lioness."

"Even better," say I. "Be my pussycat, and let me hunt you."

In reply, any one of my wives would have been purring sweet nothings in my ear, or finding her way into my arms, or cuddling on my knees.

Instead, Michal rises to her feet and starts bragging about how different she is from all of them, because of her splendid education.

"If you had a decent upbringing," says the princess, "you would have traveled to the delta of the Nile, like me, and there you would have seen, in several temple reliefs, how human remains are anointed, in preparation for burial."

"I've been rubbed with enough oil for one day, thank you very much, and I'm not in the mood for thinking about burials—"

"And I'm not in the mood for playing a kitten."

"Forget about human remains—"

"How can I forget?" she asks, trying to harden her voice, so it may sound icy again. "In Egypt they're smeared with sweet-smelling oils, not only in devotion to the dear departed, but also as a practical matter, I mean, to obscure the stench of death."

"Forget death—"

"In sealing a coffin," she presses on, "a final anointing of the mummy is observed."

"Oh well," I say, throwing my hands in the air. "I give up."

And as I turn to go Michal draws closer to me, takes a deep breath, and to my surprise wraps her arms around my body.

Boy, she smells good.

"Anointing," she breathes in my ear, "is often depicted in rather intimate scenes, I mean, between husband and wife, where she is shown anointing her spouse, as a sign of affection."

"Really?"

"Really."

And just when I start sensing that she is in heat Michal pushes me away and goes on with her lecture.

"The most famous example," she says, "is on the throne of king Tut of Egypt. If you wish, I'll find an artist, the best money can buy, to paint it on your throne."

"Forget my throne," I say, turning back to face her. "I'm ready for you, now. Come here."

Her chandelier earrings sway to and fro as she shakes her head as if to say, No. But her eyes sparkle. By her blushing I know that she knows that I have noticed it.

I put my arms around her waist, feeling how my touch excites her. It melts the last remnants of resistance. She comes, and not only that, but she clings to me.

And if not for my other wives, who happen to come into the women's quarters at just this moment, who knows... I may have invited her to my chamber.

But now, catching sight of the flash, the sharp, undeniable flash of jealousy in her eyes, I know that the moment of passion has come and gone—not only for her, but for me as well.

Shaking all over, she claps a hand on my shoulder. "I don't belong in this place," she says. "Why, why did you bring me here? Nothing good can come of it."

And turning to go, I say, "You belong nowhere else."

One voice rises to a hiss in the back of my mind. I can hear Joav, my first in command. This time I listen to the advice he gave me a long time ago, when I was still a fugitive, trying to evade her father's assassins.

"Our next king must be wise," said Joav, bowing to me. "He must think long and hard about the fate of each member of the Kish clan, because any one of them, and any one of their descendants for generations to come, can return one day to claim the throne."

To which I said, "I can't bring myself to kill Michal."

"Why not?"

"I don't love her that much."

The City on the Hill

Chapter 10

I have always enjoyed shining a light on all the possibilities—but now I fret having to choose between them. This I know: my decision must not be made lightly, because it will, without a doubt, affect many lives.

So I ask my adviser, Nathan, "Well? What d'you think? Shall I rest on my laurels, so to speak, now that I've brought an end, more or less, to the feud between our tribes?"

And before he can open his mouth I press on. "Or else, shall I charge ahead, bringing the fight outside our borders, to the Philistines?"

Nathan raises an eyebrow. "What, another war?"

"We must push back against those who attack us, those who have sensed a weakness in us while each tribe was fighting the others."

"But now," he argues, "now that we've reconciled, won't they be much more careful, even a bit reluctant to provoke us?"

"Perhaps," say I, "it's time to provoke them. Nothing unites like a common enemy! It may forge us into becoming not only a nation—but also a rising empire."

"Then, I think you know the answer," he says sheepishly, not daring to commit himself one way or another.

"I do," say I. "But I hesitate to admit it, even to myself, because of one thing: for perfect execution I would have to brace myself, and be ready to bloody my own hands, because I can't take the risk of relying on my first in command, Joav."

Nathan scratches that thin goat beard of his. It has but a few strands of hair left, which might make it a fine tool for painting.

"Indeed," he says at last. "You can't allow him to lead the charge for you."

"Nor can I divide power between him and the rest of my generals. Knowing what he did to that Benjamite, Abner, they fear he would come after them, too."

"This," he says, "is a task for you, only you."

A sigh escapes from my lips. "Alas, when it comes to war, no one but me has the wisdom to know when cruelty should be set aside in favor of a truce."

Even before leaving Hebron I start to imagine news, future news of my military offensive against our enemies. How many dead, how many wounded, how many towns conquered, how many—lost. But numbers are but a faint, remote sketch of combat, because when you face your enemy, and let your sword speak for you, the conversation is quick to become brutally intimate.

Already in my head rise the screams of victims, fleeing before me as I wield my weapon over their heads.

Then a hush would come, the unbearable, dreadful silence sprawling behind as I would go on, through pain and suffering, charging forward. Underneath me—I can just hear the sound—the hooves of my horse would start drumming, drumming upon the earth, crashing an occasional corpse, beating dust out of it.

In this landscape of scattered limbs, one blood stain after another would turn inky dark, marking the land as mine.

I remove my crown, and with a heavy heart I raise my arms, and put a bronze helmet in its place. The time for words is over, except for using them to excite my troops into following me. Come what may, victory or defeat, together we will march from one battlefield to the next.

I could dub this journey, '*The war to end all wars.*'

I tack my horse by putting the saddle on, then the girth and the bridle. I hold the reins, bounce gently in the stirrup, then swing my leg over, and sit down in the saddle. Then, with a select group of fighters, I ride out of the compound. Its gates creak to a close behind me.

What I leave back there is the past: seven years as the ruler of a single tribe. This place is too small, too provincial to serve me any longer, because now I am the king of a new entity. I am king of Israel.

The children of Hebron cheer me as I pass them. So do the women, who come out to kiss their men. All of them wave at me. I wave back, thinking I caught a glimpse of Bathsheba.

Then I realize my mistake. It is another girl, combing her long, damp hair. She bends over the iron railing of her terrace, the better to see us as we are leaving town. A minute later she, too, becomes a distant outline.

This is farewell to an era, farewell to a place. Win or lose I may never come back here again.

To Uriah, who rides behind me, and to the rest of my soldiers, I may seem busy, thrilled even, as I order messengers to be sent to each one of our tribes, with a national call to arms—but this is what I do, I like driving a multitude, even as I long to curl into a quiet corner, and linger one more hour in this place, and lose myself in thoughts, in perfect solitude.

I cast a last glance over my shoulder, at the balcony up there, at the top of my tower. By and by it becomes smaller and less defined. At long last it disappears in the distance, behind layers and layers of air, shimmering in the evening light.

The mane of my horse strokes my face as it trots ahead into the wind. I stretch out a hand to comb through it, overcoming the tight pressure of the belt, which holds my sword.

What I wish to sharpen is not its blade—but the tip of my feather.

I imagine a reflection of myself looking down at me from up there, from my balcony.

If I were still standing there, I would look around, take in the rooftop view with its peaks and vales. Then I would go back inside and dip my pen in ink.

I would press it into a scroll—vigorously here, faintly there—with my usual stroke, a stroke that drives through the spikes and valleys in the shapes of the letters at a steady slant.

In a way, this is like driving a chariot over a landscape. I would forget everything around me, and silence the clang of arms, so I might listen to my heart, and reach for that in me which is fleeting, and yet so divine.

Then, at the height of inspiration, I would scribble a few letters, a few words, and read them out loud to capture their music. An occasional dribble of ink may add a pause here and there, which is so necessary for letting a poem take shape.

I would pretend that what I have written is not about any particular woman, especially not about a soldier's wife, whose arms open to me out of every mark, every ink stain.

Now, with every move, I am rocked in the saddle. Carried forward into an unknown destiny, I dread what I may become. I fear that to ignore brutality, I would use self-deception as a shield. My heart will harden, as often happens to soldiers, and to those who bring destruction with them, those escorted by death.

Night descends. All is silent but the clip clop sound of our horses, trotting. Above us is blackness, which I navigate by an intermittent glint of stars. I must remain watchful, but I so wish I could fall sleep.

In my dream I would pass my fingers over the irregular texture of that sheet of papyrus. Examining it at an extremely close range I would feel the crushed, flattened pulp, and note each and every fiber. I would tell them apart by the subtle changes in direction and in the shades of their tone. Made out of grasslike sedge, which grows in abundance on the wetlands around the Nile river, this grain would bring to mind faraway, dreamy landscapes of places I am yet to see.

What separates me from that vision is violence.

I must crash our enemies, those around us, such as the Philistines. They have taken the opportunity to invade our villages, capture our towns, kill our men and rape our women, knowing full well that we are bleeding, that our civil war has left us weak and defenseless before them.

Not anymore! I vow to push back against them, so they start respecting us, respecting our new power. Only then will prosperity come to this land.

Farewell to an era, farewell to a place.

*

Before turning my attention to the Philistines, there is one thing I must do, and it is this: establish a new seat of power for my reign. I do not know the place for it yet, but already, I have a name.

The City of David.

I intend to build it upon newly conquered land, one that does not belong to any of our twelve tribes. It must command a view of them, so they would have to look up to it. In spite of the divisions that afflict us, this city on the hill would become a symbol of our nation, our hope for unity. And as for me, it would become my presence, my mark on history.

In search of such a place I lead my army along winding mountain roads, till at last, climbing out of a deep valley, I spot—out there in the distance—a great fortress, veiled in a fluid, bluish cloud.

This, they tell me, is Jerusalem.

Set on a hilltop, the fortress of Zion seems, to all appearances, impossible to conquer—until my spies find an entrance, a concealed way to get into the water shaft, which is where the Jebusites, who live inside the city walls, get their supply of water.

Meanwhile they send a messenger, with nothing better to tell me but this, "You will not get in here."

"Really?" say I. "Just watch me."

In reply, the messenger laughs in my face, which is strange, because normally people who fall into their enemy's hands should exercise a bit of caution.

Which tells me one thing: the Jebusites know next to nothing about me, and about my past as a fighter and a fugitive. They do not understand how determined I am, and what can be accomplished with just the right combination of will and wits.

"Even the blind and the lame," he says, with spite, "can ward you off."

Before he can finish his sentence we tie his hands behind him, and force him to lead us up through the water shaft. Having gagged his mouth so he cannot call for help, we emerge from the top of the shaft and storm into the streets.

Hoping for a new military leader to step up I call out, "Whoever leads the attack on the Jebusites will become commander-in-chief." Joab son of Zeruiah goes up first. So to my dismay, he receives the command.

In a matter of hours, the city has fallen from within.

I take up residence in the fortress, and rename it. From now on everyone calls it the City of David. I bring in designers, architects, engineers, and gardeners to build up the entire area around it, from the terraces inward, which makes people admire my initiative.

Nothing persuades them to love me like success. They say God Lord Almighty is with me.

What that means, Lord knows. Perhaps this: when they arrive at the foot of the hill, having traveled up the long, winding mountain road, and when they raise their eyes and spot the glory of sunlight playing above them, they cannot help but feel that if there is heaven on earth, this is how it would look: rays lifting the bluish cloud, and painting the walls of the city in golden hues, a touch warm, a touch cold.

I send messengers to Tyre, which is a Phoenician city, a center of commerce on the coast of Lebanon.

I offer their king, Hiram, my friendship. He agrees to send envoys to me, along with carpenters and stone masons to build my palace. It would be constructed of cedar logs, and adorned with exotic fabrics, dyed with a rare and extraordinarily expensive sort of purple, which his artisans produce from the murex shellfish. Tyrian purple is reserved for royalty. So by looking at the decor everyone would know, beyond any doubt, that here is a center of power.

Such is the way to create history, when none is available.

Even my enemies say that my kingdom has been exalted, for the sake of my people, Israel. And yet, my first wife, Michal daughter of Saul, keeps calling me a commoner. So I use my hard earned plunder to prove my nobility. I bring in elegant furniture and create splendor all around this place. I am unsure if I do it to please her or else, to show her she is dead wrong about me.

During construction I take secret pleasure at my success. I revel in the applause I get everywhere I go, to the point it makes me feel utterly sinful. But then again, who cares? A king is entitled to be arrogant, right? And as far as I know, no one gets hurt because of it!

I tell Hiram to build an office for me. He lays it out as an exact copy of my office back in Hebron, complete with a balcony at the top of the tower.

It is up in my office that I sit, come evening, and draw up my plans for war with the Philistines, and for truce with the rest of our neighbors. And it is here that I wrestle with something new to me: doubts.

I try to find peace not only with others, but also with myself. Which is the harder task, I think you know. I can set clear goals, and smooth the way for negotiations between my tribe and others, between one people and another—but when it comes to me, I find myself in darkness.

Who will show me the way?

They say God Lord Almighty is with me, but am I with Him? This is so agonizing, so hard to answer.

Perhaps I have been too hasty to bask in my own glory. I am new at this job, and to be honest, my achievements so far have been few and far between.

Should I build my palace, when I have not even started to lay plans for a temple, to recognize that mysterious power that guides my hand, and blesses me wherever I go?

I unfurl a scroll and write, "Lord, remember David, and all his afflictions. How he swore unto the Lord, and vowed unto the mighty, God of Jacob."

I read the words out loud. At the sound of them I figure that talking about myself in such a formal, removed manner, as if I am a third person pleading on behalf of the king, is a bit strange, even pretentious.

I do not waste time rewriting, but the next lines I strive to express in my own voice. I say, "Surely I will not come into the tabernacle of my house, nor go up into my bed. I will not give sleep to my eyes, or slumber to my eyelids, until I find out a place for the Lord, an habitation for the mighty God of Jacob."

I take a pause. I listen to the great silence that rolls around the entire landscape, from one hill to another all around Jerusalem, crowning me with what I long for the most.

Solitude.

And while listening for a sound, or even an echo of a sound, I pray, "Arise, O Lord, into thy rest. You, and the ark of your strength. Let thy priests be clothed with righteousness, and let your saints shout for joy. For thy servant David's sake, turn not away the face of your anointed."

The Lost Ark

Chapter 11

The war with the Philistines, fought in two back-to-back battles in the Valley of Rephaim, has come to its conclusion so swiftly that I find it rather boring to my taste. Courage is meaningful only when there is some risk of losing the battle, which is not the case this time. Nathan the prophet and Gad the seer, both of whom try to outdo each other by keeping records about my reign, have a hard time writing anything worth reading about it.

Writing history is a tough task, and not only because I avoid sharing every story with them. Granted, I have my secrets, but to be perfectly honest I rarely lie. Instead I omit a few details here and there, and ask them to bury others under a mountain of papyrus, which they do quite skillfully by compiling long lists of soldiers, commanders, tribe leaders, judges, even musicians, and by producing a pile of cross references, such as who begot whom and who died at what age and where. And to keep things simple, they barely mention women.

This time, recording military events is more pointless than ever, because here is the long and the short of it: I won.

The only part you may find of interest is this: victory was secured with tactics that came directly from a higher source—or so my spiritual advisor, Abiathar, would have me believe.

With an unexpected sense of humility I ask myself, well? Who am I to argue?

This is how it happened: before the first battle I asked Abiathar to inquire of the Lord. "Shall I go and attack the Philistines? Will you deliver them into my hands?"

"Go," came the answer, "for I will surely deliver the Philistines into your hands."

With such assurance what choice did I have but to go ahead and defeat them? My men carried off the idols left behind, and burned them, which spurred the Philistines to come back for a second battle.

Again I inquired of the Lord. This time Abiathar told me that He answered, "Do not go straight up."

"Why not?"

"Because," said the priest, "I said so! Do I need to repeat myself?"

To which I said, "I heard you the first time, but wanted to make sure I understand the plan."

"Circle around behind them and attack them in front of the poplar trees."

"Really? God mentioned poplar trees?"

"He did," said Abiathar, sliding a hand over his priestly garment, the ephod, which was meant to assure me that he knows things better than anyone, better then me.

"Any more advice?"

"As soon as you hear the sound of marching in the tops of the poplar trees, move quickly, because that will mean the Lord has gone out in front of you to strike the Philistine army."

I hesitated to ask, "Really?" again, because Abiathar might view any expression of doubt as outright blasphemy. The last thing I wished to do was clash with an extremely devout person.

I could not help but think that his plan seemed too solid, too clear, and far too elaborate. Usually his advice is ambivalent. Wrapped in mystery, it offers details that are intentionally vague, which allows him to say, "I told you so," no matter what happened. This was the first time Abiathar dispensed military advice in the name of the Lord, and the first time he did so with such exact detail.

The plan was simply brilliant. I followed it religiously, and struck down the Philistines all the way from Gibeon to Gezer, which is a major city, with a large fortress, one that dominates the crossroads of the Way of the Sea, and the road to Jerusalem and Jericho, both of which are important trade routes.

Now my victory is complete. It allows the flow of goods across the land, which would gratify the rich, and provide work for the poor.

From the south, Egyptian merchants start importing luxury items, such as toy pyramids made of white limestone. Their shape is said to represent the descending rays of the sun. I get an assortment of them, in various sizes, for my boys. From the south, Babylonian merchants start bringing in terra-cotta plaques done in high relief, depicting Ishtar, the Queen of the Night.

I get the icon, with the thought of giving it as a gift to Michal, who may like it, because she has quite a collection of idols. But then, on a whim, I decide to keep it. I find the frontal view of a nude goddess with wings, bird's feet, and a horned crown, surrounded by owls, quite compelling. I would hate to part with it, as I am just beginning to learn the cultures around me, and the meanings of their half-human, half-animal deities.

Perhaps, in the most profound sense, this duality is a symbol of where I find myself at times. I wish to reach for my angels, and at the same time, to embrace my demons.

I am not the only one delighted by such exotic goods. Our shepherds get them in exchange for leather and wool, and our farmers —in exchange for sacks filled with grain and produce, as the harvest has been particularly abundant this year.

Wherever I go I can sense hope. Men and women cannot wait to cheer, to sing, to dance in the streets—but for the time being I hold them back. There is one more thing I would like to do before announcing a celebration.

I wish to bring the chest, the sacred chest containing the stone tablets handed down the generations from our legendary leader, Moses, upon which the ten commandments were inscribed.

The Ark holds a great fascination on me, and I have my mind set on bringing it here, to Jerusalem, so as to turn the city into a spiritual center.

So I confer with each of my officers, the commanders of thousands and commanders of hundreds. Then, facing the entire assembly of Israel, I suggest the idea cautiously.

Moving the Ark is considered to be dangerous, because—if done without proper respect—it may arouse the wrath of God. How proper is proper, God knows. I suppose a lot of sacrifice would be needed.

Even the Philistines believe that just holding the Ark, or even getting too close to it, may cause horrible diseases, not to mention hemorrhoids, a plague of mice, and an affliction of boils.

With this in mind I come before the assembly. I get a clear sense of adoration from everyone, but it can quickly evaporate if I say the wrong thing.

So I start slow, I say, "If it seems good to you, and if it is the will of the Lord our God, let us send word far and wide to the rest of our people throughout the territories of Israel, and also to the priests and Levites who are with them in their towns and pasture lands—"

"Yes!" they cry, not waiting to hear the rest of what I have to say, which is as gratifying as it is annoying.

"Let's have them come," I call out, "and join us—"

"Yes! Yes, let them join!"

"And, let's bring the Ark of God back to us, for we didn't inquire of it during the reign of Saul."

"Yes! Let's do it, lets bring the Ark!"

All in all I am pleased that the task seems so straightforward to everyone. I mean, how hard can it be?

*

Captured years ago by the Philistines, the Ark was taken to several places in their country, and at each place misfortune befell them.

After seven months of moving it around, the Philistines returned it, of their own accord, to our territory. Eventually it was taken to Kirjath-jearim, a city of woods, where it remained—out of sight and for the most part, out of public attention—for the last twenty years.

My first attempt at carting it ends up a total failure. An oxen stumbles. A man reaches out, perhaps a tad too hastily, to prevent the Ark from tipping over. Upon touching it, he falls down.

Haste, it turns out, is the wrong way to convey reverence, and severely is he punished for it. To my amazement I find him struck dead, which is interpreted by all as an omen, a sign of God's wrath. Hordes of people bolt out of the place as fast as their feet can carry them, escaping with fright that could be called unspeakable, if not for the screams.

For the first time in my life I fear the Lord. I am awakened to His presence. Up to now, having overcome one obstacle after another in my bid for power, I have taken providence for granted. I have given little thought to His divine ways—only to find out how abrupt they can be.

Now, strangely enough, I become angry, very angry with Him. After all, that man made an innocent mistake, with no intent for harm. Should he be taught a lesson, in such an incurable, harsh way? For what? Is this justice? Really?

And if such is the risk I am taking, how can the Ark of the Lord ever come to me? Is the danger worth the glory?

If you see Him as a father, then I am the rebellious son.

Having failed to bring the Ark to Jerusalem I decide to wait before giving it another try. Meanwhile I cannot focus my thoughts. They stray from one thing to another. I look for something, anything to occupy them.

I find it quite by accident.

One night, unable to fall asleep, I sneak out of the palace without telling the guards. I take a long walk downhill, and find myself at the mouth of a cave, just above the Kidron valley.

I brush my fingers over the walls. By the damp touch I remember passing here before, on my way to the water shaft, as I climbed up to storm the city—but at that time I was focused on the upcoming battle, and took little notice of the beauty, the eerie beauty of this place.

Once my eyes get used to the darkness I start sloshing around, barefoot. Reminded of my days as a fugitive I am drawn inside, hoping to feel ensconced in a sense of safety.

It is here that I discover a hidden marvel.

Fed by underground water that accumulates in an even deeper cave, somewhere below the surface, a spring gushes out. Splash, squirt, stop, it spurts water every so often. I know its Hebrew name, *the Gihon Spring*, which captures its rash, intermittent nature.

First I make a note to myself to talk to my engineers, so they may redirect the flow into the valley, to water the terraced plots on the slope, which I plan to name *The King's Garden*. Then I forget all about it, because I find myself utterly absorbed in rhythm, and in the resonance of sounds around me.

Watching the cracks in the rock I listen how water gurgles underneath them, how it comes, siphoned out with a big, sudden splatter—only to be swallowed back once again.

Such is the ebb and flow of life.

Climbing up I imagined the view I would have up there, at the top of the world. And now, having achieved victory, I am beginning to come down, seeking reflection.

From outside the cave comes the hoot of an owl. Outlined against a dreamy moonlight, it strikes an upright stance, and turns its large, broad head to face me. Its gaze meets mine. At the moment I feel a strange affinity to this bird of prey. Like me, it must cherish its solitude.

And as it spreads its feathers I think I see out there, behind the flutter, a curvaceous outline of a nude. I ache to touch her flesh. It is glowing with warm, reddish hues of terra-cotta. Her breasts are tipped with gold.

As if springing to life out of some Babylonian plaque, there she stands, surrounded by owls.

There she is, my Queen of the Night.

"Bathsheba," I whisper. My voice gets lost in the vacuous space.

A moment later, the owl takes off. It rises away in its silent flight, and the illusive light of the moon starts dimming out.

With All My Might

Chapter 12

I started out having no intention of boring you with platitudes, but at this point I will, because such is my whim.

Preparation does pave the way to success.

This is what I conclude, having studied how to carry the Ark of God in the correct, prescribed manner, according to our scriptures. At my insistence, the priests consecrate themselves before approaching the Ark, and so do the Levites. Wearing a priestly gown, the ephod, one of them draws near the Ark, trembling with great reverence.

He finds the four golden rings, which are attached to its four feet. Through them he inserts poles of wood, overlaid with gold. Four of the Levites lift the poles—ever so gingerly—onto their shoulders, just as Moses commanded. The Ark bounces over the heads of its carriers. Following them come the carriers of the altar. They lift its poles of acacia wood, overlaid with bronze. Sunlight starts playing back and forth between gold and bronze.

Leading the procession I glance at road ahead, and at the crowd behind me. The scene evokes a memory, an age old memory of the Sinai desert. If not for the moist, brown soil underfoot, you could have mistaken it for our exodus, generations ago, out of Egypt. The road to the City of David is long, even longer when you worry what might happen at every twist and turn.

Determined not to groan under the weight of the Ark, one Levite says, "With great zeal, the Lord our God protects what is His."

The other one whispers, "He is known to have struck a man down for some unintended offense regarding the Ark."

And the first replies, "Heaven forbid God should do so again."

I count steps, inhales, exhales, shakes of the Ark of God over their shoulders. When they have taken six paces I raise my hand, and stop them.

"Again?" they say.

"Yes," I say. "Again."

To appease the Lord, so He may not act on a whim—or, even worse, out of hunger—I sacrifice a bull and a fattened calf. Then I let the Levites go on for the next six paces.

In His name, the soil behind us is drenched with blood.

And yet, there is an air of mystery surrounding the scene. I know, based on studying the ancient instructions, that the Ark is plated entirely with gold, and that it has a crown around it. But I cannot see it, nor can anyone else, because the Levites have covered it with a gold-threaded shroud.

Every so often I spot two outlines, right there at the top, which is when the two carved cherubim peek out from under the shroud. They look like lions with spread out eagles' wings, and with a human face. I imagine them glaring at each other, and at me too, perhaps expecting a misstep.

I hold up my hand. "Stop!"

"Again?"

"Yes. Again."

Another a bull, another fattened calf are offered to the Lord, after which I count six more steps, before raising my eyes to the cherubim once more, to try and read the mischievous, golden glint in their eyes. What more can I do to figure out His will?

If Michal were here, she would claim that these winged icons are not all that different from other deities, such as the Philistine icon of Dagon, which we usually mock for being half-human, half-fish.

We see it as a monstrous combination, but in her opinion, even a monster is easier to face than the unknown.

My first wife is an expert on local cultures, and despises that we see ours as superior to theirs. She says we pay for it with anxiety. The pagans can see who they are dealing with. Unlike them, we can never be sure. Our God is illusive. His presence can only be guessed.

In a way, perhaps there is something to what she says. Our faith is more blind than others. It is made of layers upon layers of things we can never see, let alone understand.

I look around at the people rejoicing at the sight of the Ark, and applauding me along the way, which puts me in a heightened state of reflection. I promise myself that I will never let them down. I hope that through this momentous occasion—which will allow me to create a spiritual center in my city, the City of David—I can start molding them into one nation.

One of the Levites glances at me, as if to remind me of something.

"What?" I ask, snapping out of my thoughts.

"Again?"

"Oh yes. Again."

Perhaps it is the smell of blood, together with the sense of mystery, that bring to my mind the dangers lurking ahead—not just on this journey, and not just in my generation, but in generations to come. Somehow I foresee, right here and now, how our offspring will be lead, powerless, to the brink of extinction.

I shudder to see the calf, held with a knife to its throat, fall to its knees before the sacrifice. Sharply has its last bleat died down.

Then it is placed on the bronze altar, and carefully arranged into position between all the odd implements: the pails for removing ashes, and the shovels and basins and forks and fire pans and the utensils of bronze. In a flash, its body is completely consumed by fire. Nothing but ash remains.

This burnt offering is a vision of our future.

This calf is us.

I feel an overwhelming sadness, and to escape its grip I begin to dance. I dance because this is our moment, because the future is faraway and the dangers it holds are still obscure. With enough joy, enough energy in all of us, perhaps we can change its course.

Denial is bliss.

I give it everything I have. I dance with abandon. I dance with all my might.

As we come near the walls of the city I hear shouts, cheers, and the sound of trumpets, which spurs me to cry out, to sing. And as I am singing, the gates open before me.

Sing to the Lord, all the earth
Proclaim His salvation day after day.
Declare His glory among the nations
His marvelous deeds among all peoples

*

Earlier that day I took off my royal garments in favor of wearing a linen ephod, which is an elaborate garment, worn by the high priest, woven out of gold, blue, purple, scarlet, and gold threads. What made me wear it I cannot tell, except perhaps vanity. I thought I might feel priestly, even saintly for once. But if such was my intention I must have failed miserably, judging by the comments of all those who are capering here about me.

A man kisses my hand. "Oh, David," he says, slavering over me.

Then his voice trails off, as a woman nudges him away from me. She rises to her tiptoes and wraps her arms around my neck.

"Oh Lordy Lord," she says. "In this short little gown, you look devilishly handsome."

Oh well, I say to myself. Being a saint is not in me, but let all my failures be that delightful.

Carried on everyone's shoulders I begin to feel not only devilish but on top of the world, too. I find myself utterly aroused by all this adoration, and decide that when I am back at the women's quarters in my palace, I am going to bless my dear wives, by which I mean, we will all count our blessings in bed.

It is not every day that I call all of them at once into my chamber —but if not now, when?

When my tower comes into view I hop off to the ground, and bless the people in the name of the Lord Almighty. They bow, I blow off a kiss, and without missing a beat I go on dancing with all my might, aiming for home.

Here, here I come.

And who should be greeting me upon my arrival if not my first wife, Michal daughter of Saul. Well, '*Greeting*' is not exactly the right word. It is with pursed lips that she is siting there, by the window, watching me. By the flash in her eyes I know what I have always tried to avoid seeing. The princess despises me in her heart.

"What?" I say to her.

"Nothing," she says, with scorn in her voice.

"No, really," say I. "What have I done?"

Michal curtsies before me—but the gesture is so full of mockery, and her tone so acid, more so than ever before, that I take a step back.

She says, "How the king of Israel has distinguished himself today, going around half-naked—"

"Did not—"

"Did too," says the princess. "In full view of the maids of his servants, as any vulgar fellow would!"

At first I try to offer an excuse. "It was before the Lord," say I, "that I danced."

To which she says, "Was it."

To which I lash out, with a scorn bigger and more commanding than hers. "It was before the Lord, who chose me rather than your father or anyone from the House of Kish, when He appointed me ruler over His people, Israel."

She is silent—but her eyes speak hate.

Which sparks my anger. To her I will always be a commoner. Since I cannot shake off this title I might as well wear it with pride. After all I used to be a shepherd. To my people I still am.

"I will become even more undignified than this," I tell her. "I will be humiliated in my own eyes."

"You should," she says, harshly.

"But," say I, "by these maids you spoke of I will be held in honor."

In a snap, my anger grips me. To control it I look for something, anything to distract me, which is when I note a strange thing, right there behind her, in the distance by the side of the royal courtyard.

There, in the gate leading into the newly constructed building, which is designated for various professionals serving in the military and for their families, a chubby maid is crouched. She is kneeling down before someone who is hidden from sight. Veiled by the shadow of the doorway, her mistress is unseen—all but the ruffled hem of her robe, which flutters now and then as she changes position, crossing one shapely leg over the other.

Meanwhile, sleeves rolled up, the maid is busy pouring water, in a thin stream, over the bare little foot presented to her. She is rubbing the ankle, caressing the heel of the foot, doing her job briskly, yet with great tenderness, utterly oblivious to anyone who may be standing here, watching her.

The glow of that flesh, shining through the liquid, soapy splash of light, is something I find utterly fascinating

Michal follows my gaze and her lips start to quiver.

"This," I mutter, "is utter nonsense. Just, barren talk."

"Wait," she says, as I turn my back to her. "Don't go."

"It's too late," I say, and mean it.

A sudden change has come upon her, which I no longer care to understand. The princess clings to me and her finger trails, ever so delicately, around my ear—but really, it is too late for that.

I walk away, not wanting to face the jealousy in her eyes, and the tears that well up, and the love.

*

Heading for my office I cannot help but recalling a conversation I had long ago, when I was still a fugitive, with my first in command, Joav. He was the first to call me, '*Your majesty,*' even though at the time I was known throughout the land as a common criminal.

I remember every word that passed between us. He expressed his concern about the daughter of Saul. In his opinion, the surviving members of the House of Kish should be located, and one by one, they should be eliminated, to secure the future of my house, the House of David.

I remember hesitating to agree with him.

"What you mean is, it's one thing to rise to power, and quite another to maintain my grip on it. I'm beginning to see it," I said, without committing myself to any particular action.

"What Michal carries in her womb is a danger to you," he said. "Take a stab at it."

"Joav, I owe her my life."

"Then, one way or another, make sure she is childless."

This time I promise myself that I will.

It is a harsh decision on my part. It makes me cruel in a way wars have never done, because for a woman in our culture to be childless is the same as to be without value.

You might as well be buried alive.

On one hand, this is a hot-headed decision, but who cares? With her spite—cast at me at a moment that should have been lived, savored, celebrated—Michal has asked for it.

On the other hand, this decision is based on a cold calculation. I do not want her to have my child, because just like his grandfather, Saul, he may be prone to madness.

What's more, when her son succeeds me to the throne, he may reinstate Saul's version of truth. And then, then I will become notorious for my past as a rebel, a traitor, or even worse, I will turn into a nobody. My name will be stricken out of the books, out of history.

Right now, Michal is jealous of the rest of my wives, perhaps because she hates sharing my attention. Imagine how bitter her envy will grow, year after year, when she is the only one amongst them with empty hands, and an empty womb.

Childless she shall remain, till the day of her death.

Like One of My Sons

Chapter 13

And so starts a new phase in my relationship with my first wife, Michal daughter of Saul. It is colder than cold, which makes me feel uneasy, and more than that: guilty. Up to now I saw myself as a warm-hearted man, a man whose capacity for passion can never be extinguished by brooding, nor can it be exceeded by the number of his wives and concubines.

On my way to the top I have mastered many skills, not the least of which is seduction. Now at the prime of my life I am the best of lovers, if I say so myself.

I know how to please my women, and how to let them find pleasure with me. Between taking and giving I make adjustments for each and every one of them. I can be rough or gentle, as they want me to be, in the heat of the moment. I don't mind pure lust, nor do I shy away from lust that is not pure at all.

But with the princess—being who she is—this is a different game, and both of us must calculate our moves.

So now I am careful to avoid Michal, which torments me—but not enough to choose a different way, a way to reach out to her. When by accident we cross paths—in the women's quarters or in the royal gardens—she seems withdrawn, or else she is content to leave things between us as they are.

To quiet my conscience I tell myself that being warm-hearted cannot stop me from being cool-minded. Emotions are explosive. Dark clouds may gather. Lightning may strike. Matters may foment around me, but when I reflect upon them they end up displaying themselves to meticulous examination under a clear, bright light.

So this I know: to ensure stability in the country—not only for me but for generations to come—I must do everything in my power to secure the throne. Despite her apparent weakness Michal represents a threat to it.

A little after sunrise as I go around the bend of a garden path, who should I come across but the one I wish to avoid. There she is, standing under an apple tree heavy with fruit.

Somewhere in the background rings the laughter of children. The chatter of their mothers is heard. Their rounded, pregnant curves flicker, deep down there between one strip of light and another, delineating the trunks. My wives rise to the tips of their toes to shake this branch, then another, letting the ripest apples fall into their outstretched aprons. The princess glances back at them, wraps her arms around her willowy figure, and glares at me. All I can see in her eyes is blame.

"I don't belong here," Michal says, tartly.

"You," say I, matching her tone, "belong to the house of Saul."

"I do," she says, taking a step back, as if to avoid tumbling onto truth, onto the fate that is about to befall her.

On a whim I give her one more chance. "You seem to have drifted away lately," I say. "Why don't you come one evening to my chamber, talk to me?"

She shakes her head. "I can't stand being a part of your house."

"Nothing to worry about," say I. "You aren't. Not really."

I hold myself back from saying, You never will.

But both of us can hear the unsaid.

Soul searching is such a tedious thing. I wish that by the grace of God I could stop doing it.

In an attempt to feel better about myself I try to do the best job I can outside the domestic scene.

I aspire to become a benevolent ruler. At the end of the celebration for the arrival of the Ark of God into my city I give a loaf of bread, a cake of dates and a cake of raisins to each person in the entire crowd of Israelites, both men and women.

Mind you, this is no easy matter, as the storing of ingredients and the hiring of bakers and the dispensing of baked goods must be planned well ahead of time, to prevent long lines of hungry people. I set up vendors on every street corner, every marketplace in Jerusalem.

Wherever you go, the air is infused with the sweetness of honey, mixed in with new seasonings, for which we are yet to learn the foreign-sounding names. These new spices are imported here by merchants who feel safe enough now to travel alongside the Jordan river or the lowlands by the shore.

The crowds are satisfied. The adulation I receive from them is incredible, but even that falls short of making me whole. My thoughts turn, again and again, back to Michal. To remove her from my mind I direct my thoughts to her brother, Jonathan son of Saul. Unlike her, he used to declare his devotion to me every single time we met, including our last conversation, only a few weeks before his death.

I remember: there we stood that morning, seven years ago, in a deserted field behind Saul's court. He faced me, casting a shadow longer than himself over the terrain.

I knew that his father sought to kill me. At last, Jonathan knew it too.

I said to him, "We must part ways."

And he said, "Must we?"

I pointed at Saul's palace. It seemed so magnificent to me then, so solid, and that is the way it continues to exist in my memory, because I have not gone back there to see the ruins.

"This," I said, "is no place for either one of us—but I can't take you with me, Jonathan. That would place you in even greater danger. Your father will find a way, a severe way to punish you."

"I know it."

"Stay by his side, but keep a safe distance from him."

"Go in peace, then," said Jonathan, "for we have sworn friendship with each other. The Lord is witness between you and me, and between your descendants and my descendants forever."

As soon as he uttered this last sentence, it started resonating in my mind with an odd, eerie echo.

Then, having turned to leave, never once did I look back at him—but I felt his pain, his longing for me.

Listening within to what he had said, and without to what he was doing, I heard him weeping, weeping loudly over the lingering whisper of his words. *Friendship forever... Between your descendants and mine...*

Then he mounted his horse. The clatter of hooves soon faded away.

I cherish the bond between us, and remember the promise I made him for preserving that bond, extending it so it may last well beyond us into the future. Alas, it is this promise that keeps me awake at night, because it puts me at odds with the need to eliminate the last heirs, the last survivors of the House of Kish.

With either one of these children of Saul—Michal, with her hate, or Jonathan, with his love—I end up being in the same place. Wherever I turn, I find myself torn.

I am at odds with myself.

The question of how to handle the remaining descendants of Saul lays heavy on my mind. I tell myself that in time I will come up with a solution—but whatever it may be I must first locate every last one of them.

So I ask anyone who may know, "Is there anyone still left of the house of Saul, anyone at all, to whom I can show kindness?"

At last, one of my spies says, "Well..."

"Well what?"

"I can ask around."

"I must know," I tell him. "I mean, for the sake of Jonathan, my brother."

"Was he your brother? Really?"

I hate having to explain things. So in place of saying, "Not exactly," I quote from my own lovely eulogy. I say, "I grieve for him. He was very dear to me. His love for me was wonderful, more wonderful than that of women."

"Really?"

"Why," I say, "don't you believe me?"

Which he answers by asking, "What about your love for him?"

I make a note to myself never to engage in conversations with spies, even if they are mine, because they suffer from a severe case of mistrust, which means that they know how to glean the truth even if you cover it, as best you can, with a little lie here and there.

Later that week he tells me that he has found a steward of Saul's household, named Ziba.

So I summon the steward to appear before me.

"Are you Ziba?" I ask him.

"I am," he says. "At your service."

I ask, "Is there no one still alive from the house of Saul to whom I can show God's kindness?"

I may have been hoping for a simple denial. Had he shaken his head '*No*' my life would have been simpler. I mean, I could move on to other matters of state.

But to my surprise, "There is still one soul left," says the servant. "Jonathan had a son—"

"Really? I never knew he got married!"

Ziva shrugs, not knowing why I had not heard about it. Clearly, he thinks I must have been lost somewhere in the wilderness, to miss the news. He is right. I was.

"At any rate," says the servant, "Jonathan named his son—"

"Yes?" I say eagerly, hoping that the prince named his son after his best friend. My name has such a lovely ring to it.

"Speak up!" I tell him. "You were saying, he named his son—"

"Mephibosheth."

"Mephi-what?"

"Bosheth."

I take a brief pause, mulling over the sound of it.

At last I say, "The boy would have appreciated a somewhat shorter name, and so would I."

The servant nods his head as if to say, Poor boy, he must hate his name, it's quite a mouthful.

"Tell me what you know about the boy," I say. "I'm going to bring him in, and treat him as if he were one of my own."

So the servant goes on to say, "He was five years old when the news came, I mean, the terrible news about the death of Saul and Jonathan out there, on mount Gilboa. His nurse picked him up and fled, but as she hurried to leave, the boy fell, and became lame in both feet."

When the son of Jonathan—whose excruciatingly long name is so much bigger than him—is carried in, the guards thrust open the doors of the dining hall. From there he bows down, even deeper than the servant who has escorted him. With a misshapen frame, the boy can barely be recognized as a member of the house of Kish, which surprises me.

Being an admirer of all things beautiful I have expected something different of an offspring of that bloodline. This crippled youngster has no charm to speak of, nor can he draw crowds around him by any other skill. I greet him with dismay, and so would anyone else who cares to take a look at him.

In no way can he pose a threat to me, either now or in the future. That said, I hear that he has managed to sire a child somewhere, and there is no telling what that child may look like. He may grow up to be tall and handsome, which would make him look like Saul, incarnated. That would make an impression upon some tense, restless souls, who are itching for someone, anyone to lead a rebellion against me.

Without a doubt Joav would tell me that it is reason enough for immediate action, and that he can lay his hand on this boy and on his baby, and in one fell swoop slay them both, for my benefit.

Listening to me you may think me careful, to the point of being overly suspicious.

You are so right. If I were not me I would think so too. But alas, mistrust comes with the territory.

I remember the way it tormented my predecessor, Saul. He tried to control everyone around him, by striking fear in their hearts. He did it with severe mood swings and by the explosive thrust of his spear.

Unlike him I can do it with a single glare.

Carried in closer by the guards, his grandson is deposited in front of me. I have practiced his ridiculous name a few times, so now it falls out of my mouth with ease. Rising from my seat at the long dining table I say, "Mephibosheth!"

At the ringing sound of my voice, the boy's face turns ashen, and he shudders.

"At your service," he says, with a catch in his throat.

"Don't be afraid," I say to him, knowing that in his place, I would be sprinting around the guards to find an escape. Of course, being lame in both feet, he can do nothing more than tremble.

I hope that pity cannot be detected in my voice when I tell him, "I will surely show you kindness for the sake of your father Jonathan. I will restore to you all the land that belonged to your grandfather Saul."

The boy bows his head, halfway between caution and gratitude.

"And," I say, "you will always eat here, at my table."

At this he bites his lips, to avoid saying what is on his mind, which brings back to me a vision of my own first visit to the court. In a blink, I see myself at his age, coming before his grandfather, Saul.

I remember: the king growled at me, told me to go back home to Bethlehem. So I turned to leave, and stepped into the dark corridor, which was when my eye caught a metallic flash.

Hung up there on the wall was a magnificent iron shield. I brushed my hand over the sharp ridges of the inscribed letters, trying to figure them out by touch. To this day, my fingers still carry that memory, that feel of a cold, hard surface.

The thing was polished to such a degree that in it I could catch a reflection of myself. My image danced in and out of the metal engravings, and over the inscription *The House of Kish*, as if to suggest future twists in my story, which in time would overwrite his.

Now here I am, years later, standing over his grandson, in whose eyes I can spot an unmistakable squint, as if to hide his fear.

I must have narrowed my eyes in just the same way, back then in Saul's presence. I find myself amazed that like the shadow around a sundial, time has come full circle.

The play is still the same. A boy facing an overbearing, formidable king. The only thing that has changed in it is my role.

With effort I manage to silence the stirring in my heart.

"Your place will be set, down there," I say, pointing at the far end of the dining hall.

The boy recognizes that he cannot refuse me. My offer for him to eat at my table is far from being a simple hospitality. It amounts to a house arrest. We both know that by political necessity I want to watch him, I must have him under my thumb.

Wincing in pain, he bows down before me, over his broken legs.

"You'll be like one of my own flesh and blood," I say. "Part of my family."

He is silent.

"No need to thank me," I say, in my most gracious manner. "It's in honor of your father, with whom I had a special bond, and in honor of what remains of the house of Kish."

In his fright he lets out a heart wrenching groan.

"What is your servant," he asks, "that you should notice a dead dog like me?"

I find myself unwilling to give him an answer, but to myself I say, Nonsense! Pulled out of a ruined house, even a dead dog can bring calamity over us.

Nothing is more dangerous than rotten flesh.

Meanwhile I summon Ziba, Saul's steward, and say to him, "You and your sons and your servants are to farm Saul's land for his grandson, Mephibosheth, and bring in the crops, so that he may be provided for."

I have half expected him to ask, "What, no free meals?"

But being a clever steward, he refrains from blurting out silly, unnecessary questions.

Instead he puts on his obedient expression, and says to me, almost immediately, "Your servant will do whatever my lord the king wants done."

From that day on, the boy eats at my table. Well, not exactly: most of the time he just stares into his plate. It makes for a strange mood in the dining hall. Mealtimes turn out to be very quiet. Glances are exchanged between many of my guests. They shovel food into their mouths as if it were gravel, and swallow it with barely any chewing.

He is like one of my sons, except he isn't.

A Peek at Bathsheba

Chapter 14

With or without a leader, the country is now set on its course. It is thriving during this time of peace. Alas, for me this means a new kind of trouble. Having defeated the fiercest of our enemies, the Philistines, I feel bored. Restless, too. My wives complain that all I do is yawn. They suspect that I am wearing myself out, doing things about which no one dares to speculate—but the truth is I am doing nothing of the sort. I am doing nothing at all.

Mind you, I would never admit to having mischief on my mind—but even if I did, I would avoid acting upon it because of my spiritual adviser, Nathan. Lately he has been trying his hand at being my scribe, which annoys me even more than his ministering to my needs—the way he perceives them—with his nonsensical riddles and fables. Attentive to the point of being tedious, he sits at my feet all day, every day, and follows me everywhere I go to record everything I say or do. So I do and say nothing.

And for the first time in my life, my mind wanders aimlessly, unable to settle on any particular goal.

Ambition displeases when it has been fulfilled.

Here I must mention a minor political incident. It has to do with a bad haircut, which led, unfortunately, to a full fledged show of force. When the king of the Ammonites died, his son Hanun succeeded him as king.

Wanting to establish good relations with him I sent a delegation, made up of my most qualified diplomats, to express my condolences. Hanun suspected my diplomats to be spies, which was not necessarily wrong. The wrong thing was acting on such an assumption, and doing so hastily and without proof.

His men seized my envoys. To make a mockery out of them—and by extension, to ridicule me as well—they shaved off half of each man's beard, cut off their garments at the buttocks, and sent them back here, to me. Which forces me now to teach Hanun a little lesson. One thing leads to another, and before you know it, here is a new war.

It is the end of the rainy season, which is the time when kings go off to war, because the soil has dried up at last. No longer does mud suck at your feet as you move into position, or charge ahead into battle.

But I tarry behind. In my place I send out my first in command. Afraid of becoming rusty Joav is eager to polish his military skills. In my name, he leads the army across the Jordan river and into the eastern hills, destroys the Ammonites and sets siege to their capital, the city of Rabbah. Knowing my anger at him for murdering Abner, he wants to make amends. In his mind, nothing would please me more than a new victory.

If not for my boredom I would agree with him.

Joav is confident of his capacity to conquer the city, perhaps too confident, because it holds out, somehow, under his attacks. In time, our troops may succeed in assailing the lower district on the river, but how to capture the citadel is a harder problem.

So he comes back to Jerusalem for a brief visit to seek advice from me.

Sheepish as ever Nathan opens the door for him, then crouches down at my feet, where he combs through his thin beard, waiting for me to say something smart, something worthy of recording for posterity.

Glancing at the view from the window Joav cannot help but spot a multitude of newly erected structures. Centered among them is a magnificently decorated tent, the tabernacle.

Joav points to it. "What's that?"

"A holy place," I explain. "A portable dwelling, designed for the divine presence—"

"What?" he says, rather cynically. "Nowadays, the divine presence needs a shelter? From what, from wind? Rain?"

And when I am slow to answer, he says, "Ha! Here was I, making a mistake—out of ignorance, I'm sure—of thinking that God floats every which way, in the wind, in the rain, everywhere."

I hear Nathan shaking his head as if to say, Shame on you.

I tell Joav, "It's for us more than for God, a place to worship Him. People have a hard time dealing with the abstract."

"Ha!" says Joav. "They must have an icon set before them, a golden calf, or something. I bet they pray there, before the Ark—"

At that Nathan raises his head from his scroll. "That's blasphemy!" he blurts out. "The Ark is a holy object. Don't you dare compare it to calves of any kind, golden or otherwise." And holding his pen like a weapon he goes back to his silence, and to scribbling.

Meanwhile, doing my best to be patient with my first in command, "It's a temporary place, Joav," I say, "until a temple is built."

"And the altar of burnt offering," he says, "is it in there?"

I look at him, utterly in surprise, knowing that he is far from being religious. "Why," I say, "what d'you care about it?"

Under his mustache he conceals a sly smile. "Ha! I know all there's to know about the altar," he says. "It's a place of refuge for fugitives."

"And you, you'll need it one day," I mutter, as a sudden rage overtakes me.

I bite my lip to stop myself from saying anything more. I see him in my mind back there, in Hebron, piercing the soft belly of Abner, right there under the rib, which he did in peacetime as if it were in battle. I imagine the belt around his waist getting stained, and the sandals on his feet getting drenched, up to the ankles, in his victim's blood.

"Yes, don't I know it," says Joav, with a penetrating look, as if he can see through my silence. "One day you'll want me dead."

I say nothing.

He twists the end of his mustache, and gazes at the tabernacle. "When that day comes," he says, "I would run in there, to seek asylum."

Nothing continues to be my answer.

"I would take hold of the horn," he says. "I mean, the brass horn in the corner of the altar. Without it there would be no place, for someone like me, to escape your judgment."

I meet his gaze and hold it. Meanwhile I go on saying nothing.

His eyebrows stand bushy over his steel-grey eyes. "Will you forgive me then, your majesty?"

Nathan chants to himself as he writes, "Will you forgive me then," after which his pen stops, it hovers in midair, expecting the sound of my reply. I take my time fumbling around my desk, looking for maps of the eastern hills.

Meanwhile Joav presses on. "When that day comes, will you grant me a pardon?"

"Let's talk about something else," say I.

Joav holds out his hand. "Wait," he says. "One more thing."

"What?"

"Why is it so low?"

"The tabernacle? Why, I made sure it's built according to precise specifications, recorded by Moses generations ago, back at the time of exodus, and—"

"Perhaps so," he says, cutting in. "But see here, the top of the thing is well below your window."

"So?" I shrug. "Am I to blame if my supplier, Hiram king of Tyre, decided to raise the level of my tower, for no better reason than he had an overstock of marble blocks and cedar logs?"

"In your place," Joav says, "standing here, right over what shelters the divine presence, I would feel above God."

"Enough with that," say I.

On second thought I suggest, "Let's talk about something else. Yes, let's talk about what we're here for: conquering Rabbah."

"I give you my word." He claps a heavy hand over his chest. "Next time I come back I'll bring you the crown of their king."

"I have a crown," I say carelessly, waving my hand at him. "What do I need with his?"

"His is bigger than yours."

"What does that mean?"

"I hear it has countless gems embedded all around it," says Joav. "Gems he obtained—one way or another—from the crowns of other kings. It's sparklingly glorious! You'll like it. I promise."

"It won't fit. His head is bigger."

"When he loses it I'll fit it on yours."

Pointing at the open trunk next to my desk, where an assortment of crowns of all sizes is displayed left and right of the sword of Goliath, I tell him, "Sure, why not. I'll add it to the collection."

He says, "Come join me, join our forces. It'll be fun."

"No," say I. "This time I'll have to rely upon you."

In reply and in parting he says, "I won't disappoint you."

"I have no doubt about it," I say, drearily.

And drearily does Nathan echo, "I have no doubt about it."

And so I stay behind in Jerusalem, for no good reason other than a distaste for joining him, and for fighting.

*

One evening I awaken to the sound of birds, chirping. I get up from my bed and walk around on the roof of the palace, where a red-rumped swallow is trying out its skill in a courtship song. It is springtime. The hills around my city roll in and out of green. The trees beacon me from afar, bearing their blossoms.

Through the decorative lattice that marks the edge of my roof I see a woman, an achingly beautiful woman bathing on a close-by roof. She has just wrapped herself with something translucent, so her body is hidden from sight—all but a distant impression of her foot.

The first time I saw Bathsheba, back in Hebron, happened seven years ago. Luckily, at that time I had no historians in my employ, which is why that incident has gone unnoticed, and unrecorded in the scrolls. It remains known to me alone, and to her.

At the time I doubted she had caught sound of my footfalls. I edged closer, advancing stealthily along the shadow, a seemingly endless shadow cast across the flat surface of her roof. Never once did I stop to remind myself that such behavior is unbecoming of a king.

And who could blame me? In her presence I was reduced to a boy.

I brought my crown along, simply to impress her, even though it sat somewhat uncomfortably on my head. It was a bit too large for me, and too loose, too, because it had been fashioned to fit the skull of my predecessor, Saul.

On my way I leapt across a staircase, leading down from the roof. On a railing, there in front of me, was a large Egyptian towel, laying there as if to mark a barrier. I told myself, This isn't right. I should stop, stop right here and whatever happens I should cover my eyes, avoid taking a peep at her.

Should I turn back?

And immediately I answered by asking, What? Stopping midway is nothing short of a sin. You would never forgive yourself.

To which I replied, stop talking to yourself already! Are you out of your mind?

Alas, now things are much more complex. For one thing, I have more wives, each one of whom keeps an eye on me. For another, Nathan tails me wherever I go. His goat-like beard is like a second shadow behind me.

With him around, there is no way I can pay her a visit. And bringing her to my chamber would be just as impossible.

Unless...

I send him out on some unnecessary, highly urgent errand, and call in my chief bodyguard, Benaiah, a man whom I have hand picked for this job because of his valiant feats on the battlefield, which require a mind endowed with a special brand of stupidity.

This time I need him not for his courage but for his discreteness.

I point in the direction of her roof, intending to ask him something, but for a spell another vision washes over me, and I recall how alluring she looked back then, at a much closer range.

In the patches between the soapsuds, her skin seemed to glow. The rays of the setting sun were playing all over her creamy flesh, kissing one nipple, then the other. They were touching here, caressing there, sliding around her waist, poking her in her belly button, where she was chubbier than I had expected, and where the shadow sank a tad deeper.

I remember handing her the towel, which forced me to adjust the crown, because it was dancing on my head.

In profile, her lashes hung over her cheek, and the shadow fluttered. Bathsheba brought her hand to her lips and ever so gently, blew off a bubble. It came off the palm of her hand, then swirled around in the evening breeze, becoming more iridescent until its glassy membrane thinned out, and then—pop! Nothing was left but thin air.

Now, despite being an illustrious king, I am nothing to her. Perhaps, thin air is all she remembers of me. Perhaps I alone cling on to that moment, unable to forget it.

From this distance I can barely see her. Wrapped in a long robe, which is made of some shimmering fabric, the only flesh visible to me is her little foot.

From afar I must look too small to her. Perhaps all she can see is a flash, a sudden spark from the corner of my roof as a ray of sun catches my crown. Perhaps she spots a dark shadow slanting into a window in a distant tower, one among many windows, many towers, and to her it seems still, which is why she ignores me, and goes about the business of smelling one piece of soap after another, and rubbing them on her skin.

I glance sideways at Benaiah.

"Tell me," I demand, as if I have spotted her now for the first time, "who is that woman?"

He squints, the better to see her, and says, "Oh yes! She is Bathsheba, the daughter of Eliam and the wife of Uriah the Hittite."

"Go knock at her door," I tell him, "and give her this note."

He comes back awhile later.

"Done," he reports. "She read it."

"And?"

"Nothing."

"Nothing?"

"Was she supposed to say something?"

"Why wouldn't she?"

He shrugs.

I groan.

"Shall I run back?" he asks.

Benaiah earned his fame as a war hero, and he killed a lion in a snowy pit, but as a go between in a simple exchange between the sexes he is utterly useless.

"Bring her to me," I command. "But be sure not to be followed."

At that, his mouth drops open. On second thought, he gasps.

"If I'm not to be followed," he says, "how can I bring her?"

"Be sure she's the *only* one following you." I roll my eyes at having to spell things out. "This is between me and you."

"Oh," he says. "And Bathsheba too, right?"

"Yes." I lower my voice. "It's going to be our secret. No one but us is to know about this, especially not Nathan."

Having sent my spiritual advisor on his errand and Benaiah on his mission I run down to the King's Gardens and back up again, bringing with me a huge bouquet of freshly picked Jasmine flowers, which fills my chamber with a sweet fragrance. It is then that time takes a strange, unexpected turn. It slows down.

I have no idea how much of it I have wasted since the beginning of my wait. All I know is that it feels without an end.

And despite knowing that I have arrived, that I am at the prime of my life, I feel, once again, like a teenager. She loves me, she loves me not. With a flick of my wrist, white petals start scattering across the marble floor.

I go out to the roof and pace to and fro. Already, there is chill in the air. The rays of the setting sun give a last flicker before darkness, before a sensation of fear sets in. Then they withdraw, hesitating to touch the tabernacle of God down there, below me.

Coming back in I set the twin sconces, left and right of the chamber door, aflame. Which is when, to the quickening of my pulse, I see it opening.

There she is, lifting her little foot and setting it across the threshold.

Love

Chapter 15

Wrapped in a long, flowing fabric that creates countless folds around her curves, she loosens just the top of it and lets it slide off her head—only to reveal a blush, and mischievous glint, shining in her eye. It is over that sparkle that I catch a sudden reflection, coming from the back window, of a full moon.

Looking left, right, and down the staircase, to make sure no one is lurking outside my chamber door, I let her in. Then I lock it behind her, so no one may intrude upon us.

In a manner of greeting I raise my goblet. It is a gift from my supplier, Hiram king of Tyre, and unlike the other goblets I have in my possession, this one is made of fine glass, with minute air bubbles floating in it. With a big splash I fill it up to the rim with red, aromatic wine. In it I dip a glistening, ruddy cherry, and offer it to her, with a flowery toast.

"For you," I say. "With my everlasting love!"

Bathsheba takes the goblet from my hand, and raises it to her lips. "Love, everlasting?" she says, raising an eyebrow. "What does that mean, in this place?"

I hesitate to ask, "What place is that?"

"This court," she says, with a slight curtsy, "where the signature feature is a harem, which is as big as the king is endowed with glory."

"Glory is a good thing," say I, lowering my voice. "But sometimes it is better to meet in the shadows."

"Especially," she says, matching her voice to mine, "when there are so many others."

"Here we are," say I. "It's just us."

"Really," says Bathsheba, sipping her wine and ever so delightfully, licking her lips. "It must be a special night, then! Just you and me, and no one else, no one else at all."

Yet I cannot avoid feeling the presence of someone other than me in her thoughts, perhaps her husband, Uriah, who is one of my mighty soldiers and the most trusty of them. Earlier today he must have received his transfer orders to join the cavalry in the eastern hills, where he would be stationed outside the city of Rabbah.

I refuse to imagine him pressing her to his heart, kissing her goodbye before a long departure. Am I merely a distraction? I wonder if she misses him already, if she thinks of the dangers he would face.

I have a catch in my throat as I tell her, "I'm so glad you came."

Bathsheba lifts her eyes and looks straight at me.

"Really," she says, in her most velvety tone. "You mean, I had a choice in this matter?"

Her question stumps me at first, because how can I admit that she is right, so right in asking it? Instead I just shrug.

"You do have a choice," I say at last. "And I hope you'll make it."

"I'm so glad to hear that," says Bathsheba. "With that ape, I mean, that bodyguard of yours knocking so loudly, so rudely, and for such a long time at my door, I had my doubts about it."

"You can go, if you wish," I stress, with a reluctant tone. "But I wish you wouldn't. Stay with me, tonight."

Bathsheba picks the stem of the red cherry, and takes little bites out of it. In her pleasure she hums, and smacks her lips. Then she raises the goblet to my lips, letting me take in the aroma. I do, and then I take a long gulp.

With a slight sway of her hips Bathsheba walks past me, knowing I cannot take my eyes off of her. She wanders about my chamber as if she were the one owning it.

"You've been brought here by my order," I whisper to her, across the space. "But I am the one held captive."

I sit at the edge of the bed, utterly fascinated by her beauty. Her lashes are long, they flutter over her cheeks, and her hair waves around her face with the rhythm of her steps. It glows like copper under the flaming sconces, but when she crosses in front of the window it turns blue against the moonshine.

She glances at the collection of crowns, down there in my trunk, and leans in to touch some of them, perhaps to estimate their sizes, and the number of nations, the number of kings I conquered.

"Fine pieces," I say, casually. "You can choose as many of them as you want."

"No," she says, drawling the word until it turns into a sigh. "I'm bored with it."

"Are you? Bored with jewelry?"

By way of an answer she says, "After every battle Uriah brings me a little something, which he chooses for me out of the plunder, hoping I won't refuse it this time."

"Which you always do," I say, half-asking.

"I have no use for such things."

"Then, what is it you want?"

"Who knows," she says, vaguely.

Aroused, this time by curiosity, "You must know," I say.

"But," she says, teasingly, "I'm not going to tell you. You, of all people, would never understand me."

"Why not?"

"Because," she says, waving a hand at the open trunk, where my treasures are strewn about, and at my bed.

"Because what?"

"You've been blessed. You possess so much that you can't begin to appreciate your luck. So many things, so many victories, women, children."

With that, she bends over a pile of maps and other scrolls of papyrus.

Pushing them aside, Bathsheba fingers the surface of my desk, where my firstborn child, Amnon, carved a little face—perhaps of his half-sister, my precious baby, Tamar—into the wood. Bathsheba strokes the childish, uneven sketch, and brings her hand to her lips, cherishing the touch of it.

And it is then, at the sight of a tear welling in her eye, that I ask myself, What does this wooden surface, scarred as it is, mean to her? Is she moved by the expression of love, or by the face of a baby?

After so many years of marriage, with a husband as doting as Uriah, she is still without child. And with her reputation—about which she can do little, because she is, after all, a soldier's wife—Bathsheba must have been with many men before me. Still, she is childless. How else can you explain this fact, but by assuming she is barren?

For other women this is a curse, but for her—for both of us—this may be a blessing in disguise. If she opens her arms to me and takes me in I would not have to be careful with her. We would take pleasure in each other, without having to worry about the consequences.

Bathsheba reaches for my lyre, and plucks at the strings. All of a sudden something trembles in the air, a strange vibration bemoaning loss, agony, longing.

It is to that sound that I take a long, swinging stride into her. She rides it out. And so, with no need for words, we start swaying in and out, out and in, to the dying echo of the music, which by now is heard only in our heart.

A long, wavy strand of hair spills over her bare shoulder. I comb it back with my fingers, and ever so briefly stroke her neck. Her lips brush against mine—but only for a near touch, which leaves me wanting.

Now she shimmies the fabric off her other shoulder, takes a step away from me, and turns to go out, onto the roof.

I gather a few large, soft pillows from my bed and carry them outside, that we may recline upon them.

I set them down by edge of the roof, close to the vine of roses, which is twisting over the wooden lattice and into it. Between its diagonal slats I see a black void gaping upon us, dotted by a magical glint of starlight.

Separated from her by the thought of a kiss I sense her heat, and the gust of air scented by roses and by her flesh—but I cannot tell if the breath between us is hers or mine. Which is when I know, for one perfect moment, that she is part of my essence.

I am part of hers.

Bathsheba holds me in a tender embrace as I lay her down. Scattered petals fly off, swirling in the air around her long, silky hair that starts cascading here, over the pillows and onto the tile floor.

Accidentally the goblet, which she has set down next to her, tips over and some of the wine spills over her hip. I dip a finger in the red puddle beside her, and paint countless grapes around her waist.

Intoxicated I murmur to her, "Your graceful legs are like jewels, the work of an artist's hands. Your navel is a rounded goblet that never lacks blended wine."

I want to wait, wait for her to give herself to me—but in the end I cannot fight my passion any longer, and I take her. She sighs softly and arches against me, rising on the fervor of my caress, higher and higher into ecstasy.

What wakes us up when the glow goes out of the stars, when they hang over us like stones, and the hills around us take a faint, still uncertain shape, is a sound.

Dazed, we look up at the heavens as if we were underwater, sunken and floating with the stream, and what startles us out of our dream is the march of soldiers out of the courtyard below, and the clinking of swords.

In alarm Bathsheba opens her eyes.

"Stay awhile longer," I whisper to her.

"And live here with you," she counters, "happily ever after?"

Before I can think of an answer Bathsheba rises to her feet and walks to the edge of the roof. Peering out through the lattice, "Nay," she says. "Both of us know that's not going to happen."

It is sunrise. Sprawled around us is the city, its hills drifting in and out of grayness. Sudden gusts of wind press against newly erected scaffoldings, near and far. The tent of God can be seen below, its tissues alive, blowing like a mouth, a huge mouth swelling and puffing in unspoken anger.

It brings to mind what my first in command, Joav, said to me. "Standing here," he said, "I would feel above God."

The troops march around the tabernacle, snap to attention when they reach its front, and bow deeply. Then they file out onto the road, heading east to the faraway city of Rabbah.

I unlock the chamber door, glance left, right, and into the stoney shadow of the stairwell. To my relief my scribe, Nathan, is nowhere in sight. I give my hand to Bathsheba. First we move on our tiptoes, slowly, carefully, like little children playing hide and seek. Then, in leaps and bounds, we run down the stairs.

Near the bottom, where the staircase twists onto the landing, I am feeling particularly reckless. When she sets her little foot—a bit precariously—on the last triangular stair, I pull her to me. Wild and carefree I hope we can both slip.

I find myself loving risk of all things—even more than her—and not minding anymore if a glimpse of us can be caught through the opening, as we lie there one last time before it is over, before both of us are forced to come out and lie, lie to ourselves, lie to everyone else, pretending that last night never happened.

"This," I say, closing my eyes, "Is happiness."

"Yes," says Bathsheba. "For one night, it is. With the power you have, be sure not to make it the cause of mourning."

For some reason I hold myself back from asking her what she means.

All too soon Bathsheba gets up, dusts herself off, and straightens the folds of fabric about her. Then she walks out into the blindingly bright sunrise, her eyes clouded with some thought, perhaps worry.

There is one thing, one nagging notion I am beginning to form in my mind as I watch her going, and it is this: yesterday, when I wrote her that note, I knew I was tempting Providence. What I failed to consider was the fact that she would be the one to suffer the consequences, more so than me.

*

For a whole month, fearing that a scandal may erupt, I avoid sending for her. It is the beginning of summer, and the heat is unusual, unrelenting—but I avoid going out onto the roof, which is where a light breeze can offer some relief, because it is there, more than any other place, that I ache for her. I whisper her name, and burn up at the mere sound of it.

I try to take control of my desire by playing my lyre and writing poetry, but notes and words fail me. Everything I compose these days seems to be but a pale shadow of a shadow of what Bathsheba means to me.

And the one image that keeps coming back to me is our reflection in the glass, where our faces melded into one. My eye, her eye, and around us, the outline of a new, fluid identity. A portrait of our love, rippling there, across the surface of the wine.

But I keep asking myself, with the same tone as hers, "Love, everlasting? What does that mean, in this place?"

At the height of the lunar cycle, when the moon grows full once again, I give in to temptation. I go out onto the roof, where I hope, in vain, to catch a glimpse of her. And just as I start agonizing, asking myself how long can our secret be kept silent, an interruption occurs.

My bodyguard, Benaiah, comes out. I want to believe that he knows nothing about me except what orders I give him, and how I want them obeyed.

When he comes to a stand near me I spot a note in his hand. I recognize it: this is the same little papyrus scroll I sent with him that first time, a month ago, but she must have sealed it anew.

I break the seal and then, then I stare at the unfurled thing, utterly speechless. It takes just three words to get me into this state.

In long, elegant glyphs, Bathsheba has written, simply, "I am pregnant."

Uriah

Chapter 16

I must keep myself away from her, to protect both of us from gossip. In secret I send word to Bathsheba, to let her know that I intend to take care of her. I want to do the right thing, one way or another—even though I have no idea, at first, what that may mean. What action should I take? Should I reunite her with her husband, or else take him out of the way, somehow, and make an honest woman out of her?

Utterly baffled I close my eyes. I try not to think about the forbidden woman, not to imagine her nude—but my mind works against me.

There she is, sitting in her bedroom, crossing one leg over another at the edge of the bed. By her side, over the richly embroidered, velvety blankets, lays her robe. It is damp and crumpled, because in my mind she has just come out of the bath. From somewhere above soft, golden light is washing over her, letting her flesh glow against the darkness. Light glances off a teardrop earring that is hanging from her earlobe.

I pay no attention to the maid, who is kneeling there before her, because she is barely seen, sunk in the shadows of my vision. Instead I focus on imagining Bathsheba. I paint her face turned from me, in profile. She is holding back a tear as my note rustles in her hand, with the whisper of my word of honor.

By the look in her eye, she senses that which I have not yet begun to consider. With profound sadness, she can already foresee the calamity, which my promise would cause for her, and for her husband,

Uriah. In my mind Bathsheba is already grieving—and yet, she seems to accept her fate, the way I would dictate it.

I wipe my eyes, to make her disappear. My confusion starts to border on a sense of panic.

I find myself feeling guilty one moment, and the next moment blaming everything on my trusty soldier, Uriah. I hate him, I mean, I love him, I do—but as a doting husband, he should have been more careful.

He should have kept her out of sight, so her beauty would not tempt me. If you think this is a harsh thing to say I agree with you—but then, consider this: by the law of the land I am above the law.

As wild as this sounds I did not invent it, quite the contrary! This principle was declared with great clarity by our prophet, over a generation ago. He warned our people that a king would be entitled to have any woman he fancies, for any purpose, any whim whatsoever.

Samuel said, and I quote: "This is what the king who'll reign over you will claim as his rights: He'll take your sons and make them serve with his chariots and horses, and they'll run in front of his chariots... He'll take your daughters to be perfumers and cooks and bakers."

I am—am I not—above the law. Not so Bathsheba. With every passing month of pregnancy, she would become more vulnerable, because in our culture, adultery is punishable by stoning.

How vividly I recall my father warning me about the possibility of this turn of events, using lofty, overblown proverbs, which had been passed down to him a generation ago, by his father.

"My son," he said, "be attentive to my wisdom. Incline your ear to my understanding, that you may keep discretion, and your lips may guard knowledge."

"Yes, dad," I said, hoping to sound obedient.

"The lips of a forbidden woman drip honey," he said, which intrigued me.

"Really?" said I.

"Yes," he said. "And her speech, it's smoother than oil, but in the end she is bitter as wormwood, sharp as a double-edged sword."

"You mean, sin cuts both ways?"

"I mean, a forbidden woman is sin itself. Her feet go down to death. Her steps follow the path to hell."

Even back then, as a child, I could not make up my mind if to accept his guidance or ignore it, because really, if temptation is such a sweet thing, how can it be all that bad?

Seriously now: injustice irks me, especially when it is directed at the weak among us, and especially at women. It takes two to engage in this particular type of sin, does it not? So why should the woman bear the entire blame?

And when the time comes, am I supposed to pass on this questionable wisdom to my own children—or else, should I impart to them my own, untraditional sense of justice?

Of all of them I am thinking now of the one Bathsheba carries in her womb. He would be born of a forbidden woman, out of sin. Are my father's proverbs the right kind of teaching for him? Would he become so high-minded as to carry them forward, to his children?

Is it the right kind of teaching for any one of us men, born of women?

I straddle many of these questions, because I am wary of hypocrisy. My first instinct is to protect Bathsheba from overly righteous gossipmongers.

True, her marriage to Uriah has been interrupted, on occasion, by his military service faraway from home. Even so, there were plenty of chances for them to make love. So no one knows, no one understands why Bathsheba has not conceived all these years. Tattlers may have assumed she was barren, as I have done, to my own detriment. But maybe the problem was not her. Maybe he is sterile.

So now I ask myself, will people accept the child she carries in her womb as his? To which I answer, well, God knows! Stranger things have happened!

A plausible timeline must be constructed to support such an improbable outcome. I figure I must bring her husband back here at the earliest opportunity so he may make love to her. Who knows, he may even rejoice that at long last, she is in the family way.

If all goes well, he will claim the baby as his, and step into the role he deserves: that of the fool.

I have the best of intentions, and cannot help but feel benevolent, and so proud of myself for setting my own interests aside. This entire plot has been conceived to preserve her family life, such as it is. If not for having to cloak it in secrecy I would expect someone to flatter me for it, and sing high praises for my sacrifice, because clearly, in spite of wanting her in a really big way, I will have to distance myself from her —at least in the near future.

So I send word to my first in command, Joav, all the way to the capital city of Rabbah. "Send me Uriah the Hittite."

And Joav, bless his soul, asks no questions. He sends him to me, with the tacit understanding that clarifications are unnecessary, because they stand in the way of action.

For that I am grateful to him.

*

When Uriah comes before me he seems unusually tense. His jaw is set, his face—pale.

At first I figure that the long journey to the city of Rabbah and back here again must have drained him. I try to ignore the pain I detect in his eyes. I mean, it must be my mistake, I am seeing things. And whether I like it or not, for his wife's sake I must push him into a trap.

For that I do feel guilty.

Even so I must make sure he goes home. Bathsheba will know what she must do, once he is there. No woman is more skilled than her in the delightful art of seduction.

I imagine she will wash his feet from the dust of the road, and rub his aching muscles, each and every one of them, and take it from there.

I force myself to engage him in small talk, which feels uncomfortable to both of us.

I ask, "How's your commander, Joav?"

Uriah says, in his Hittite accent, "Fine."

"And the other soldiers?"

"They're well."

"How's the war been going?"

"Not bad."

"Not bad, huh?"

"No, not at all."

"That's good," say I. "Really."

Nothing more remains to be said. I wonder if he wonders why I have pulled him out of a critical battle, and brought him back here, to Jerusalem, only to engage him in a polite chitchat, over nonsense such as who or what feels fine, well, not bad, and good.

Trying to break an uneasy silence I tell him, "You must be tired. Go down to your house and wash your feet."

Uriah snaps to attention and leaves the palace, after which I send my bodyguard, Benaiah, after him, with a gift: a platter of succulent cherries and a casket of red wine, that he may loosen up and have fun with his beloved, loving wife.

Next morning I step into the court, hoping to turn my attention to pressing political and social matters, such as controlling some unrest on our border with the Sinai desert, and holding a series of meetings with ambassadors from Babylon, Egypt, and Moav, and dealing with an unexpected shortage of materials for a new wing for the palace, and consulting with city designers and architects, in order to select the most appropriate site to build a temple, and in the midst of all of that, separating between my boys, Amnon and Absalom, who are at each other's throat.

And just as I rise to my throne my bodyguard, Benaiah, comes in to tell me that my trusty soldier never made it home last night.

"What?" I cry. "How dare Uriah disobey me? What a scoundrel! What a fool! Doesn't he know that his wife's expecting him—"

"He knows she's expecting."

"What d'you mean by that?"

"Mė?" says Benaiah, wearing his innocently dumb expression. "Nothing."

"Where did he sleep, then?" I ask.

"At the entrance to the palace," says Benaiah. "With all the servants. No matter what I told him, he refused to go down to his house."

As Uriah is summoned back to the court I ask myself, why is he so obstinate, so determined not to visit his wife? It is possible that a hint, a rumor of his her adultery has already reached his ears? If so, is there any course of action open to him? I mean, what can a soldier do to defy a king?

When he comes before me I ask him, "Haven't you just come from a military campaign? Why don't you go home?"

Uriah the Hittite says to me, "Your majesty, the Ark of God is staying in a tent."

"What? Have you become Jewish all of a sudden?" I ask. "I mean, what is it to you, where the Ark stays? You can go to your house and have a merry good time, and forget living in a tent just because God does."

"How can I forget?" he asks. "My commander Joav and my lord's men are camped out there, outside Rabbah, in the open country. How can I go to my house to eat and drink and make love to my wife? As surely as you live I'll not do such a thing!"

Then he grows exceedingly quiet. By the look in his eyes I see what he thinks. The only way open to him is silent resistance.

I feel for him, because I know how it feels to be in his shoes, simply by remembering my years in the court of my predecessor, king Saul. With a shriek, his spear would come singing straight at me.

I remember: depending on how close it came I would catch the thing—or else dodge it, letting it hit the wall. It would hit hard, then fall bouncing to the stone floor. The entire space would fill with echoes of it, ringing.

"Here," I said, picking it up, returning it dutifully to Saul.

"Boy," said the king, watching me with a crazed look in his eye, as I went back to my place behind him. "What would a king do without his jester."

Now, even without hurtling a spear, I am the one using Uriah for my jester.

I decide to give him one more chance to redeem himself in my eyes before I give up on him, before I begin to despair of my own redemption.

So I tell him, "Stay here one more day, and tomorrow I'll send you back."

He remains in Jerusalem that day and the next. I invite him to eat and drink with me, which allows me to take a stab at trying to make him drunk.

I slap him on his shoulder with a fine sense of camaraderie. I even give him my goblet. I fill it for him so it is overflowing with beer. He gulps it down dutifully. One keg after another is brought in. Meanwhile I discuss how it is flavored with hops, which add a hint of bitterness, and act as a natural preservative, and how during the process of fermentation, herbs may be added to one keg and fruit to another, for no better reason than achieving variety in taste. By the end of the evening I am exhausted by all this talk, and so, I think, is he.

After all this effort on my part I am astounded to learn that nothing, nothing at all comes of it. Uriah goes out in the evening to sleep on his mat among my servants. He is steadfast in refusing to go home. Perhaps he fails to understand that being stubborn may cost him dearly.

Next morning I sit down at my desk to write a letter to Joav. “Put Uriah out in front,” I write, “where the fighting is fiercest.”

I take a deep breath, dip my feather in ink and shake it, that it may not bleed.

“Then,” I go on writing, “withdraw from him, so he will be struck down and die.”

I seal the scroll and give it to my dear, trusty soldier, knowing he would never suspect he is carrying his own death sentence in his hand.

And for a long time after the sound of his steps has died down I remain there, sitting at the edge of my throne, listening for him, hoping he would come back to me, wishing I could find a way to save him.

Outside my window I hear thin voices of children. They have marked the ground with chalk, and are hopping joyfully about, singing.

Uriah went to Rabbah, because you told him to.
He left his wife behind
Because his trust was blind
You brought him back from Rabbah, to drink a lot of brew.

*

An entire month drags by. I have no idea how I manage to hold myself together, nor do I know how Bathsheba is doing. By overhearing a conversation between my wives I learn that she has been seen in public, in one of the market places. For her sake I pray that her pregnancy does not show yet.

And I am ashamed to admit, even to myself, that I hope for the worst. Whatever fate befalls her husband, it must be decisive.

If he gets merely wounded, and is brought back to Jerusalem along with other soldiers who have lost their limbs, who have become shadows of their previous selves, then... Then, there would be no doubt in anyone's mind: the baby cannot possibly be his.

At long last I am told that a messenger has arrived at the palace, carrying news from the capital city of the Ammonites, Rabbah.

He falls at my feet, bearing a grim expression on his face.

I demand, "What's the news from the front?"

Quaking before me he says, in a meek voice, "Your majesty, forgive me! This time, what I have to report is far from joyful."

"Why, what happened?"

"The men of Rabbah, they overpowered us, they came out against us in the open, but we managed to drive them back to the entrance of the city gate. Then, then their archers shot arrows at your servants from the wall, and—"

"Slow down," I say. "Take a pause, organize your thoughts. Now, let me ask you this: Why did you get so close to the city to fight? Didn't you know the Ammonites would shoot arrows from the wall?"

"This," he mumbles, "is just what Joav said you'd ask."

"As my first in command," say I, "he should learn his lessons from our military history. He should know about the battle of Thebez, several generations back."

"Joav told me all about it—"

Over his interruption I say, "During that battle our leader, Abimelek, led an attack on the besieged city. He fought most of the way towards the tower, then drew too close to its wall. And then, then a woman on a high point of it dropped a millstone upon his head. The blow cracked his skull—but unfortunately, didn't kill him. He called his young armor-bearer, and asked him to draw his sword and run it through him, so no one would know, no one would laugh at him, as his demise had happened not by crossing swords with a mighty soldier, but by the soft hand of a woman."

"Joav, he knows every one of these details."

"Then why, why did you get so close to the wall? He should have known better! Did he prepare you with any kind of an answer?"

Trembling, the messenger says, "What he told me to say, your majesty, makes absolutely no sense to me. I doubt I should even repeat it."

"You're testing my patience," say I, casting a look of warning at him. "Tell me exactly what he's said."

He shakes his head, saying, "I beg you, my lord. Please forgive me. I should just say nothing, nothing at all, lest you would have me put to death."

"I'll do no such thing, given a reasonable answer."

"Reasonable, I'm afraid, it's not. What's the wisdom in explaining one calamity by dropping in a mention of another?"

"Just quote what he told you to say and I promise I will not hold it against you."

The messenger looks up at me with worry in his eyes, as if he is not entirely convinced by my promise. "Joav said to me, 'When you've finished giving the king this account of the battle, his anger may flare up. If he asks you this, then say to him, 'Moreover, your servant Uriah the Hittite is dead.'"

"Uriah is dead?"

"He is, my lord."

He mistakes my silence for grief, and goes on to condole with me. "I'm so sorry to tell you this, knowing how much you loved him," he says. "Please, please forgive me."

I give a deep sigh, knowing that my relief can be disguised by it as sorrow.

For a moment I am speechless, and utterly impressed by how cleverly my first in command executed my order. History repeats itself. Joav used it, quite brilliantly, to my advantage. He sent Uriah into a dangerous position, just below the wall of Rabbah, hoping that someone, like that woman in Thebez, would drop a millstone upon him.

And so, my trusty soldier fought his last battle. Perhaps, at the last second—as the arrow was singing in the air, coming closer and closer at him, like a lover eager for a kiss—his eyes started to widen.

Perhaps he knew that his death would not be caused by that arrow, but by the hand of a woman, the one he loved.

I tell the messenger, "I'm sorry to hear it, truly, I am."

And he says, "I'm sorry to have to tell you about it."

And I say, "Joav must be beside himself with anger at this loss. Say this to him: 'Don't let this upset you. The sword devours one as well as another. Press the attack against the city and destroy it.'"

Glad that he has escaped punishment for his report, the messenger opens the door and steps out of my court. Which is when I hear that song again, as the children have just come out into the courtyard, and are hopping over marks of chalk. They are making up new words, but the tune is the same as it ever was.

Uriah went to Rabbah, he didn't want to screw.
The man who sent him there
Knew it wasn't fair
To have his soldier die, before his pay was due.

*

When Bathsheba hears that her husband is dead, she weeps for him. Because of her pregnancy there is little time for that. As soon as the shortened mourning period is over I have her taken to my house, and let my wives know that she will be joining them without delay.

I do my best to feel elated. This is the woman I want. With a passion as delightful as ours, we are meant to be together. What a pleasure it would be to enjoy her company in the open, even in daylight! My delight, such as it is, would be marred by only one thing —but to my relief it would happen rarely enough as to allow me a chance to ignore it, ignore the haunting words.

Every once in a while I think I hear that ghastly song, drifting into my chamber through the open window:

Every time at midnight Uriah's shakes his bones
Singing for his wife
Grasping for a knife
Looking blindly for the man who placed him under stones.

The Widow Bride

Chapter 17

My first mistake today is getting out of bed.

I mean, really! As soon as I get up, and the newly installed cedar planks start creaking under my feet, the door cracks open, and who leans in but my first wife, Michal daughter of Saul. The tower of her hair comes into view first, as if to give me a warning signal before she sails in.

"Are you alone?" she asks.

To which I say, "Not anymore."

At first glance she looks like a boy, because of those thin, scrawny arms that hang by her side. Only at second glance do I notice that time has not been kind to her. Her body is at once too flat and too wrinkled, which is an impossible combination, but there it is.

"I can't stand that new woman you brought in," she hisses, through pursed lips.

"You mean, Bathsheba? Why, dear, what's the problem?"

"She's pregnant. I'm not."

"That," say I, "is because you never let me close to you."

"True," says the princess. "You don't deserve me."

"I knew you'd see reason."

"Bathsheba has grown too fat, too soon," she says. "And what's more, you give her too much attention."

"Truly," say I, "I resent you saying that. I give you all the attention you deserve."

Michal gives me a look.

So I say, "What?"

"Nothing," she says, giving me a false hope that this conversation is over, after which she complains, "you spend too much time with her."

"Not just her," say I.

To which she says, "Tell me about it."

On her way out, she gives a little curtsey to someone who is waiting there behind the door. At first, all I spot is the tip of her nose.

"I'm not disturbing you, my lord, now am I?" asks my second wife, Abigail.

"No, darling," say I. "Come right in!"

"Are you decent?"

"Who, me? D'you have to ask?"

"Well, are you?"

"I am," say I. "Come in, sweetheart. I confess, there's no one I miss more than you this fine morning."

"Oh, stop it," she says, stepping in. "My lord, you have the sweetest tongue."

"You trying to seduce me?"

"Is that a difficult thing to do?"

"Oh my," I say. "I think you are!"

"Not in the least," says Abigail, shaking her head for added emphasis—but in a blink she is blushing, as if she were a maiden.

I give her a big hug. "You sure?"

"My lord," she says, "you have that woman, Bathsheba, for that. In fact, she's the reason I'm here."

"Well? What about her?"

"I don't think she'll be happy here. Let her go back to her house."

"There's no one there," I say. "You may not know it, because you're blessed to live here, in the palace, amongst so many women, so close to me—but think about it: Bathsheba is alone. It's not easy to deal with emptiness."

"Even so," says Abigail, in a stubborn tone. "Send her back."

"I can't."

"You won't."

I look Abigail in the eye and tell her, “Dear, I intend to marry her.”

Withdrawing from me, “I see, my lord,” she says, with a slight shrug. “You intend to do the right thing by her.”

“Thank you,” I say, “for your understanding.”

“Far from it.” Abigail sighs. “I can’t see what you plan to get. She’s a nobody.”

“Which is what I used to be, not so long ago. It is a tough role to play. Don’t make light of it.”

“Worse than that. She’s a soldier’s wife.”

“And what’s wrong with that?”

She hesitates before blurting out, “She, she isn’t pure, if you know what I mean.”

“So?” say I. “Neither were you!”

Which brings her to a pause.

After a while she comes up with, “You have more wives that you can handle.”

“Even so,” say I. “Being my second wife, you’re in position to help set my house in order. She is here to stay, so why won’t you set an example for the others, and embrace Bathsheba—”

“Even if I wanted to, they would resist her.”

“Then tell Michal, Eglah, Ahinoam, Maachah, Haggith, and Abital that they’ll have to get used to her presence. I mean, one more, one less, what’s the big difference?”

“None of them,” she says, “will forgive her for stealing your heart.”

I wave my hand at her, and say, “I care little for all that nonsense. I stand firm—”

“Very good,” she says.

To which I say, “Thank you, Abigail.”

“I didn’t congratulate you,” she says. “And neither will they.”

Trying to appease her I reach over and give her a little peck on the forehead, and through pressed lips I murmur, “We shouldn’t be fighting.”

To which she replies, “It’s your fault.”

“Am I such a bad husband?”

"D'you have to ask?"

"Why shouldn't I?"

"The worst," she says, with a strained smile. "That's what you are."

I bend over my treasure box, fumble about for something nice, and give her a gold necklace. At first she smiles.

Then she takes offense, for some reason, and throws it in my direction, as if to spurn my attempt at generosity. The flush in her cheeks is the only thing that still reminds me of the first time I saw her. When that vision comes to mind, it does so with the sweet smell of pastries.

I remember: Leading a band of hungry, desperate men through the rocky terrain of mount Carmel, I looked up the road. A train of donkeys came into view opposite from us.

It was heading our way. Heaped upon their backs were baskets filled with freshly baked loaves of bread, enormous skins of wine, five dressed sheep, bags of roasted grain, cakes of raisins and of pressed figs.

And leading this procession, a red-cheeked woman rode her donkey side saddle. From a distance she looked like a sack of potatoes wearing an apron, a flowery, ruffled apron suffused with a tantalizing smell: honey and butter mixed together.

The way to a man's heart is through his stomach, and Abigail knew it. I told myself, here is a woman who knows how to handle a man. And I let her handle me—if you know what I mean—for the duration of an entire evening. Which led, one way or another, to the untimely death of her dear husband, Nabal, and to my asking her hand in marriage, which happened immediately after his burial.

She must have been happy to rid herself of him. So to my delight, the obligatory mourning period was punctuated with hugs and kisses. Nabal must have been turning in his grave to hear us dancing all the way to his treasure box, which is now mine. Oh, what a merry widow she was!

If anything, Abigail of all women should have some understanding, some compassion for what Bathsheba is going through—but I suppose that somehow, she denies the connection between my past with her and my present with Uriah's widow.

Alas, seeing history repeat itself is none too easy, especially when you are no longer the main player in it.

This is one lesson I hope never to experience for myself.

*

A year ago, the chief architect for my palace became overly inventive, which is something I welcome. He suggested to embellish the look of my tower by adding an external staircase, with each stair projecting outward from the wall—which would be seen by everyone, from every hill surrounding the city, no matter how far. At the time I thought it was a good idea, because that would leave the internal staircase as a private approach to my chamber, to be used by me alone.

I approved his plan, because as a poet I enjoy solitude, and as a politician I need to relieve myself—on occasion—from the pressure of dealing with the crowds.

Once constructed, I found it offered one more advantage, which I had not foreseen before. The staircase put those who climbed up to my office on public display. It helped make them know their place once they got here.

For the most part, this works in my favor.

Since many of those who come happen to be of the opposite sex, my interest in them becomes truly notorious, whether I deserve it or not. For a king, this is not a bad thing. Depending upon whom you ask about it, my virility is hated, envied, or else, much revered.

So now when Bathsheba, my new bride, comes to me from the women's quarters, she does it the same way as the rest of my wives.

Bending over the sill of my chamber window I spot her clambering up, slowly and heavily, around the tower.

She stops for a minute to wipe her brow, because the heat of this summer is more intense than usual. Short of breath, she holds one hand on the iron railing, and the other around her belly. On her, the climb takes its toll.

Bathsheba lowers her eyes and gives a shy, hesitant nod to one concubine after another, as they are coming down, measuring her top to bottom, and flinging their skirts about, with a happy whistle on their lips.

That uneasy scramble to the top has the questionable effect of humbling her. By the time she arrives, there are tears in her eyes.

"What's the matter?" I ask, because I truly feel for her. Being an outsider, she is greeted with suspicion by the rest of my wives.

Asking this question is, without a doubt, my second mistake of the day. For a long time Bathsheba is silent.

At long last, "Oh, nothing," she says, biting her lip.

So hard does she do it that her lip becomes white, and it bears the marks of her teeth.

"Come here," I whisper to her.

Instead she goes to the window. I find myself unable to say anything, so instead I make a note to myself, to write down these words, later: "*The fragrance of your garments is like the fragrance of Lebanon. You are a garden locked up, my sister, my bride. You are a spring enclosed, a sealed fountain.*"

By the reflection I can read her. I see that she wipes the corner of her eye. Silk curtains start swishing. They sway, they billow wildly around her, blotting and redrawing the curves of her silhouette.

I join her by the window and hold her, rocking her gently in my arms. Together, we look out at the last glimmer of the sun, sinking.

Our touch is magical. It melts away the bitterness in her. I hum a sweet melody in her ear. She closes her eyes and so do I. There is no need for words, because both of us know, we both understand the hardship she has to go through in my court, and both of us know she has to go it alone.

If I would try to put in a good word for her, it would miscarry. I mean, it would be construed as favoring her to others, which would put her in even greater isolation.

I do not know if Bathsheba can find her way up from the bottom of the hierarchy down there, in the women's quarters. It takes a special skill to survive, to persevere is spite of any and all obstacles. It takes grit.

Trust me, I know all there is to know about it. That determination, graced by the joy of taking risks, allowed me to challenge men stronger than me, and rise to power in their place. And to this day, it helps me hold on to it.

Does she have it in her? Can she take on women more established than her, such as my first wife, Michal, and my second wife, Abigail? Can she gain their support, and climb over their shoulders into her own power?

Time will tell.

I love the fullness of her figure. I love her soft voice, humming the same melody with me. Most of all I love expecting the birth of our child, imagining it together with her. This is something new, which I have never experienced before. Up to now my wives' pregnancies, and the births of my children, have all gone unnoticed by me, as matters of state have taken precedence, demanding my time and attention.

I am surprised at how eager I am to hold the baby in my arms. I simply cannot wait to bend over the crib and pick him up. Or her. For me, this is going to be a long wait.

Bathsheba guides my hand, ever so gently, so I can feel her soft skin, her warmness, and the faint kick of the baby inside her. Then the glow vanishes, and in the smoky darkness we can no longer guess the exact place where it has happened.

Early next morning I get word that she is in labor. I send the best midwife in my service to her, because none of my wives would guide her through the delivery. They just stand aside, watching.

As of this hour the baby is not born yet.

For the first time in my life I have a sense, a complete sense of happiness. I am a father. In addition to my daughter, Tamar, I have sixteen boys. Their names are engraved over my desk, because there are so many of them: Amnon, Chileab, Absalom, Adonijah, Shephatiah, Ithream, Shobab, Nathan, Ibhar, Elishua, Nepheg, Japhia, Elishama, Eliada, and Eliphalet. Now here comes a new baby. I trust his future, and my destiny.

I am blessed.

A Poor Man's Lamb

Chapter 18

I have spent the last couple of days listening to several disputes between farmers and shepherds, mediating between them or declaring my verdict, as the case may be, in the hopes of leading by judging, which used to be a well honored tradition, practiced in our tribes in a bygone era, before my predecessor, Saul, was anointed king. Because of my seemingly relaxed demeanor, no one in the court could guess how eagerly I have been waiting, perking my ear to catch any signal, any word about the birth of my child.

During this wait I have been enjoying a new pleasure, that of not seeing my spiritual advisor and scribe, Nathan, around me. Perhaps he is ministering to the needs of someone else, lately.

I pity that poor soul.

Don't get me wrong: I like attention, I do—but his is a bit much. I cannot stand him breathing into my nose, right here next to me, and snatching words from my mouth even before I have the chance to sound them out. If given the choice I prefer to have some space, some opportunity for mischief, and even more importantly, for solitude.

Up to now I have thought nothing of his absence, and figured that for a change Nathan must have been busy writing his own memoirs, throwing in some rants about life in the shadow of glory. I imagine him hungering to find the words, just the right words, and like a kid, chewing the tip of his quill and the corner of his papyrus scroll.

So this morning, it is with sudden dismay that I find him there, in the court, waiting for me.

Nathan looks different somehow, but at first I am at loss to define what it is exactly that I sense about him, except to say that the sheepish look has vanished from his eyes.

"The Lord," he says, in a grave tone, "sent me to you."

"Your presence," say I, on my way to the throne, "is greatly revered. I always thought you were God-sent."

"No kidding," he says.

"Sure," say I, with a roguish grin. "No kidding."

His face reddens, and so does the wattle hanging down from his neck. He waves his quill about, which makes the bite marks on its tip dance in the air, to the point of whizzing.

"What I'm bringing before you today," he says, "is a serious matter. Stop laughing."

"Then," say I, "seriously shall I deal with it. Stop chewing that tip."

"The last thing that will help you," he warns me, "is making fun of me."

For a moment I am tempted to blurt out that the last thing I need is his help, because invariably, kings are at odds with men of God. I mean, how do you deal with someone who thinks he is holding the divine presence, and its absolute wisdom, right there in his grip? Is that why he shakes his fist at me?

I keep these thoughts to myself, because if I do not, he will write them down for posterity, and make me look more naughty than I wish to be remembered. I remind myself that I am a lucky man, a man in the prime of life, able to keep myself in fine balance against any and all adversaries.

So I control myself enough to ask him, "What is it, Nathan? What's the matter?"

"A certain—shall we say—dispute came to my attention," he says, trying to relax the tension in his voice, trying to sound casual.

I repeat, "A dispute?"

"Yes," he confirms. "And I'm not sure what to think of it."

"Tell me about it, this is what I'm here for," say I, in a grand tone.

"Is it," he says.

"Yes," say I. "My prime goal in ruling this nation is bringing about not only peace, but justice, too! Come now, tell me all about it."

Nathan gives me a sidelong glance through his droopy eyelids, clears his throat, and then says, "There were two men in a certain town..."

"Which town, exactly?"

"Does it matter?"

"Why shouldn't it?"

"Just because."

"The devil is in the details," I insist. "I like to get them straight."

No longer can I call him meek. Nathan sets his jaw firmly, and the muscles under the scattered bristles next to his ears start to tighten. Even his goat-like beard looks pointier than it used to be.

"Who knows where the devil might be," he mutters, in an unusually irate tone.

"Where he is," say I, "God knows."

He stammers. "Will you let me tell you what happened, without all these interruptions? This isn't easy for me, you know."

I motion for him to carry on, which he does. He clears his throat again, which sounds a bit like a goat cackle, and rolls the quill between his palms with great energy. He even hops from one foot to another.

"So," says Nathan. "If this sounds familiar to you, it is because it's true. One man was rich and the other poor. The rich man had a very large number of sheep and cattle, but the poor man had nothing, nothing at all except one little ewe lamb he had bought. He raised it, and it grew up with him and his children. It shared his food, drank from his cup and even slept in his arms."

"Really?"

"Really. It was like a daughter to him."

"That last bit," say I, "may sound a bit strange to some folks."

"But you can understand it, can you?" he asks, hanging his eyes on me. "I mean, you know how it is, because you were a shepherd too, once upon a time."

"A shepherd," say I, "I still am."

"Indeed," he says. "That you are."

"Yes." I agree, mainly to reassure him. "I know how it is."

He twiddles his thin beard between his thumb and forefinger, and leans over to me, breathing in my face, to the point that it is too close for comfort. I lean back into the cushion of my seat.

"Now a traveler came to the rich man," says Nathan, "but the rich man refrained from taking one of his own sheep or cattle to prepare a meal for him."

"That," I say, "was quite measly of the rich man. Did he have no sense of hospitality?"

"Oh, quite the contrary! To his guest, he is hospitable enough—but not at his own expense. Instead of choosing one of his own herd, he took the ewe lamb that belonged to the poor man and prepared it for the feast."

At that I find myself burning with anger, which amazes me, because usually I keep a certain coolness about me, especially when I pass judgment. In spite of myself, something about this particular case touches me in an surprisingly intimate, tender way, which brings me to the verge of erupting.

"As surely as the Lord lives," I cry, "the man who did this must die!"

"Must he, really?"

"And, and he must pay for that lamb three times, no, four times over, because he did such a despicable thing and had no pity."

As soon as the words leave my lips I find them a bit confusing, because if that man dies how can he possibly calculate the price, let alone pay it for the lamb?

But before I can sort out my own verdict so it may be better meted out, Nathan straightens his back, tilts his head backwards, and looks down his nose upon me.

Then he raises a trembling hand, and points it. With a clear, unmistaken expression of blame, he points it directly at me.

"You," he says, harshly, "you are that man!"

"What?" I ask, and suddenly my eyes open, which is when I get it, without needing an answer.

I understand why he has concocted this tale. No longer can I guard myself from learning a lesson. For my benefit, Nathan has cleverly disguised the facts—only to reveal the truth.

In spite of myself I admire him for presenting his fable in a way I could not have expected. I wish I could forget this made-up play. I wish I could deny the real identities of its actors. I abhor my role, my horrific role in all that has happened.

It is with magnificent pathos that he says, "This is what the Lord, the God of Israel, says: 'I anointed you king over Israel, and I delivered you from the hand of Saul. I gave your master's house to you, and your master's wives into your arms. I gave you all Israel and Judah. And if all this had been too little, I would have given you even more.'"

Hoping he does not hear the sudden catch in my throat, "No need," I mumble. "I know how blessed I am, I do."

He gives me an inquisitive look, and puts his hand against me, as if to test how stable I am on my feet. It reminds me of something I learned long ago, as a child: once a goat discovers a weakness in a fence, it will exploit it repeatedly.

"Why," says Nathan, "why did you despise the word of the Lord by doing what is evil in His eyes? You struck down Uriah the Hittite with the sword, and took his wife to be your own."

I try to harden myself against his poking, so once again I refuse to accept his accusation.

"No, no," I insist. "I loved Uriah. He was like a brother to me."

"Then, you should've protected him, even from yourself."

"Am I my brother's keeper?"

"Are you not?"

"I didn't strike him down."

"Yes, you did," he says, with great strain, great sadness in his voice. "You killed him with the sword of the Ammonites."

At the sound of his words, something comes over me. An invisible hand is squeezing my throat, harder and harder still, till I cannot utter a single word. Instead I do that which I never imagined I would. I fall to my knees before him.

"Now, therefore," says Nathan, as if the voice of God comes through him, "the sword will never depart from your house, because you despised me and took the wife of Uriah the Hittite to be your own."

I am overcome. I am broken by truth. Tears well in my eyes.

"This," he says, "is what the Lord says: 'Out of your own household I am going to bring calamity on you. Before your very eyes I will take your wives and give them to one who is close to you, and he will sleep with your wives in broad daylight. You did it in secret, but I will do this thing in broad daylight before all Israel.'"

I lower my head, and tears wash over me. Words tremble on my lips. "I have sinned," I utter, with barely a breath left in me.

I close my eyelids, and as darkness descends upon me I find myself searching for a glimmer of light, and praying, "*My hope is in you. Save me from all my transgressions. Do not make me the scorn of fools.*"

After that I wish Nathan would say nothing more. Let him just turn away and leave me here, in my agony, because nothing more needs be said. At this point I have embraced both the responsibility for my crime, and the punishment for it—even if I cannot grasp it, not yet.

And I wonder, who will it be, the one who is close to me, the one who will sleep with my wives in broad daylight? When will this happen? This, to me, is more than a punishment. It is a curse, because from now until this calamity comes into being I am sentenced, each day anew, to suspect every man, every child, born and unborn, all around me.

What is the point of begging, "*Do not make me the scorn of fools.*" I am doomed. And the most humbling part is knowing, deep down in my heart, that I deserve it.

Tormented by regret, I hear Nathan go on with his talk. To my surprise he declares, "The Lord has taken away your sin."

That, I warn myself, has been much too easy. He must be lifting me to hope—only to strike me down with an even harsher penalty.

"You aren't going to die," he says, and puts his hand on my shoulder, in the manner of giving me a blessing, almost. "But—"

"But what?"

"Because by doing this you have shown utter contempt for the Lord," he says, "the son born to you shall die."

Is the Child Dead

Chapter 19

Later, when the hired midwife comes into the court, glee in her eyes, to let me know that my wife, Bathsheba, is waiting for me with a healthy baby boy in her arms, I shake my head, which is not an easy thing to do, because it is gripped tightly between the palms of my hands. Unable to utter a single word I send her away.

Let me stay away awhile longer. Let me wait until evening—or better yet, until next morning—before going to visit the women's quarters. I cannot bring myself to let Bathsheba see me this way, drowned in confusion. I cannot place my doubts, my fears on her shoulders, not only because after two days of a complicated delivery, she must still be in pain—but because now, even in her weakness, she is stronger than me.

Let me give her a chance to recover. Let me try to heal.

The last thing I want to do is come before her and, out of distress, make the mistake of blurting out that which Nathan has told me.

"The son born to you shall die."

I step out into the courtyard, and gaze upon the tent of the Lord, which is pitched out there, opposite me. A pillar of cloud seems to be swirling just outside its opening. Perhaps it is merely an illusion, a memory of a memory of our exodus, of the way we were, way back when: guided by faith, fearing sandstorms, kneeling before dangerous gusts of wind that sweep across the Sinai desert.

Perhaps it is an apparition, conjured by light slanting through a gap in the overcast heaven—or else, it is an oddity of my own tortured mind.

I wipe my eyes, to clear my mind and see things as they are. The tabernacle has ten curtains of fine twined linen, and of blue and purple and scarlet yarns, with cherubim skillfully worked into them. They are flapping fluidly in the wind, soaring overhead.

Looking up at the peak of the tent I feel small. In my devastation I find myself praying, "*Hear my cry for mercy, as I call to you for help, as I lift up my hands, toward your Most Holy Place.*"

When at long last I head for the women's quarters, my mind is firmly made up not to tell Bathsheba about my worries, the thoughts that cloud my mind. After all, people believe that I am a man after God's own heart. Let me trust it too. Let me try to persuade Him to forgive me, or at least to spare my child from a punishment that should be inflicted on me alone.

There is an old saying, which my father relayed to me a long time ago. *'The fathers have eaten sour grapes, and the children's teeth are set on edge.'* At the time, he admired the wisdom of it. I thought it was questionable.

To me, it made absolutely no sense. My brothers must have thought me rebellious, even arrogant, for casting doubts on an age-honored phrase. They admonished me, saying, "Things that outlive us must be revered."

To which I replied, "In spite of you, and in spite of everyone who thinks like you, I believe one thing: the fact a saying is old doesn't make it worth repeating."

Perhaps I can convince Him that for once, I am right. Who knows. Perhaps I can, somehow, overturn my fate.

*

For now, the last thing I want to share with my wife is any mention of my conversation with my scribe, Nathan. So it is with great dismay that I spot him right there, standing by her bedside, next to the little crib.

Exchanging a glance with me he bows before her. Then, turning away, he drops his last words behind, in a manner of quick departure.

"God stores up the punishment of the wicked," he says, "for their children.'"

Bathsheba strains to raise herself on her elbows. "Let Him repay the wicked," she says. "so that they themselves will experience it!"

I flash a look at him, so Nathan gives up his search for an answer, and with a slight nod aimed at me, he retreats.

Once he is gone I ask her, trying to conceal my alarm, "What was that all about? What did he tell you?"

To which she says, as casually as ever, "Oh, nothing, nothing at all."

"Really?"

"Really."

Then, on a different note, she adds, "I think Nathan likes me."

Which makes me straighten my back and narrow my eyes at once, not only because I find her suggestion interesting, which I do—but because I am starting to suspect her demeanor. I mean, Bathsheba seems too calm. Overly talkative, too. Perhaps, she is trying to stir the conversation away from that *nothing*, that void she wishes to avoid.

Let us not trip into that hole. Let us not tumble onto truth.

She repeats, "Honestly, he likes me. I can tell."

"Really?" say I. "He does?"

"I doubt he'll admit it, but yes," she replies. "And, guess what?"

So I say, "What?"

And Bathsheba says, "He's promised to include my name, right there in his scrolls. To him it's a big deal, because not many women are granted such an unusual honor, in a history written by men, for men. Can you believe it? He came here thinking I would be grateful to him for that."

"Why wouldn't you be?"

"Would you?"

"D'you have to ask?"

"Why shouldn't I?"

I roll my eyes. "Alas," I say, "Nathan writes about me more than I care to read."

"You ignore what he writes?"

"Most of it. He's much too productive."

Bathsheba waves her hand at me. "Oh, admit it!" she says, with a soft, bubbly laughter. "You enjoy it, you thrive on it! Every bit of it: the extravagant praises he heaps upon you, along with the occasional mention of your naughty little affairs."

Guilty as charged, I find myself smiling. Alas, she knows me all too well.

"But," she goes on to say, now in a serious tone, "let me ask you this: would you be grateful for the mere mention of your name, if it were done without quoting a single one of your psalms, without describing a single adventure in which you engaged, or any one of your valiant military victories?"

At this I counter, "At this point I would rather he stopped writing about me altogether. For that," I say, darkly, "I would be grateful."

Bathsheba raises an eyebrow.

"Not I!" she counters. "I would like to have more than a mere mention of my name."

So I promise, "I'll talk to him. Nathan can be persuaded, with a bit of royal guidance, to add a few more details, such as your father's name."

"I've already persuaded him to do that. '*Daughter of Eliam*' will be added to the scriptures, with no mention of my mother's name, of course, because really, what does that matter in a man's world?"

"Anything else?"

"Yes," she says. "'*Wife of Uriah the Hittite*' will be added as well. D'you mind?"

"No," say I. "Not at all. He is part of you, of your past."

"Sometimes," she whispers, "I still hear him, at night."

"You do?"

"Yes," she says. "I think I hear him hiss my name, especially when the wind weeps outside."

"Let's talk about something else," I suggest. "Even about Nathan."

"Yes," she says, collecting her thoughts. "Nathan. Lets go back to him. Instead of trying to understand who I am, he finds it sufficient to write about my looks."

"He does?"

With a slight yawn, she says, "I find it so boring, don't you?"

"No," I must admit. "I don't."

Bathsheba throws up her hands. "Men!"

In reply I catch the palm of her hand and kiss it, in my most gallant manner.

"Nathan," she says, "he's a strange old man. He is tickled pink to think that I was bathing outside, on the roof of my house. He's looking for the words, just the right words to describe what he imagines."

"He better not ask me for help."

"I doubt he will. Nathan prefers his own juicy little speculations. He's suggested to me that I did it for no better reason than to attract your attention."

"Well?" I ask. "Weren't you?"

Bathsheba gives me a mysterious half-smile, as if to imply that between the two of us, no answer is necessary.

Then she adds, "He claims that my name alone will inspire many creative minds. Countless artists, he says, will try to capture that moment, the moment you laid eyes on me. They'll do me from every possible angle."

For a moment I find myself dumbfounded.

"That," says Bathsheba, "was a private moment. It belongs to me, and to no one else."

"And to me, too," say I. "I mean, how could I possibly resist you?"

She mutters, once more,"Men!"

"Women," say I. "Why don't you understand your own power?"

"Power?" she repeats. "What power?"

"I mean, the way your beauty affects us. It's too much, even for someone like me. So don't blame me if I'm forced to take a peek."

"Look all you want," she says. "Just know this: there's more to me than meets the eye."

"I know it."

"In the future," she says, "a million eyes will continue to explore me, through the eyes of those artists. Not that I mind, really."

"But I do!"

"Here is what irks me," she says. "There's more, much more to who I am than beauty alone."

At this point I utter a sigh, and in spite of myself the sigh deepens, because all of a sudden, regret is catching up to me.

"I so wish," say I, "that my scribe, Nathan, would leave both of us alone."

"Why," she hesitates to ask, "is there something you want to tell me?"

I shake my head. "No, no. Not really. And you?"

"No," she says, lowering her eyes. "Nothing at all."

I sit down beside her, and brush a strand of hair from her damp forehead. Only now—by her pale face and the dark circles under her eyes—do I realize how exhausted she must be.

"Perhaps," I say, thinking aloud, "I should be going."

Pointing at the crib by her side, "Help me now," says Bathsheba. "Give me the child."

And so, leaning over the crib, I take a look at him. His face is perfect, angelic. A single ray of sun cuts across his ashen cheek, leaving his eyes in the shadows. Along its diagonal way, it touches the tips of his delicate, nearly transparent fingers. I lift the baby into a kiss.

Then, very gently, I place him into her embrace. Standing back I watch the two of them, mother and child.

She bares her breast and brings him in, tilting herself into his little mouth, but the baby is too sleepy, it seems, to suck her milk.

I get up, and walk away to the sound of her voice singing a melodious lullaby, at the end of which it trails off, ever so tenderly, into sadness.

*

During the next few days, rumors start spreading around the palace, throughout the city, and across the entire land, saying that the Lord has struck the child that Uriah's wife has borne, and that he has become ill.

The two of us, Bathsheba and I, react in opposite ways to the scorns hurtled at us, and the and ill wishes whispered behind our backs. Fighting for the life of her baby, she holds back her own pride, and asks each one of my wives for advice. With a great burst of energy, she tries to feed him at all hours, day and night. When the little one refuses her milk, she dabs a drop of it on his lips. She gives him a lukewarm bath to break his fever, and takes him outside to the courtyard, for a breath of fresh air. There stands my love, with the baby in her arms, in full view of the tent of God.

Meanwhile I have closed myself off, away from contact. Alone in my chamber I plead with the Lord for the child. I fast and spend the nights lying in sackcloth on the floor.

"*My God, my God,*" I groan. "*Why have you forsaken me? Why are you so far from saving me, so far from my cries of anguish?*"

The elders of my household knock at my door. They come in and stand there beside me, and try to get me up from the floor—all in vain. To their surprise I refuse to talk, nor would I eat any food with them.

They leave. Again I find myself alone, and utterly lost.

"*I am a worm and not a man,*" I cry, beating my own chest. "*Scorned by everyone, despised by the people. All who see me mock me. They hurl insults, shaking their heads.*"

On the seventh day of his life the baby stops crying. I go to see him one last time. He is still breathing, but barely. I hold his limp, feverish hand in mine, kiss it, and bow my head. Tears stream down my face and fall over his, on their way to the earth.

Back in my chamber, all three of my attendants come in. I sense that they are afraid to tell me what has happened. The moment is tense, it is hard on all of us. I know what is coming.

I hear one of them whispering, "While the child was still living, the king wouldn't listen to us when we spoke to him."

And the other asks, without expecting an answer, "How can we now tell him the child is dead? He may do something desperate."

And I ask, without inflecting it as a question, "Is the child dead?"

From the corner of my eye I see them exchanging glances between them. I raise my head, and look each one of them in the eye.

At last, "Yes," says one of them. "He is."

Strangely, the hammering of my heart starts to subside. It is not as hard as it has been these last seven days.

I get up from the floor. I wash, put on lotions and change my clothes, after which I go into the tent of the Lord and worship. Then I return to the palace, into the royal dining room. At my request they serve me food, and I eat.

One of my attendants cannot help but ask me, "Why are you acting this way?"

To which I wonder, "What d'you mean? What way is that?"

"Forgive me for asking, your majesty," he says. "But while the child was alive, you fasted and wept. Now that the child is dead, you get up and eat?"

I answer, in a veiled, ambiguous way, "*What is crooked cannot be straightened. What is lacking cannot be counted.*"

"Excuse me, your majesty, what does that mean?"

"While the child was still alive, I fasted and wept. I thought, 'Who knows? The Lord may be gracious to me and let the child live.' But now that he is dead, why should I go on fasting?"

He looks at me as if to suggest, Out of sorrow?

"I mean," say I, "can I bring him back again?"

The attendant lowers his eyes and bows down. He is still somewhat puzzled, even annoyed at the way I have been stricken with sorrow—only to remove it from me with such apparent ease.

So am I.

"I will go to my child," I try to explain, even to myself, with a grave tone. "But he will not return to me."

From there I go down to the women's quarters, to see Bathsheba. The two of us continue to react in opposite ways to what has just happened. While I have regained my vigor, she has lost hers. I find her lying there, on the ground, utterly motionless.

Meanwhile, my wives have gathered around her. Some of them are whispering amongst themselves, others—wiping a tear.

In between them, light falls on her, catching her hand. By the glistening you can tell it is damp, because she is gripping her breasts, where the pain is the worst. Her milk is still welling up in them, still flowing. She is silent, but her body is still screaming for the child.

The notion of giving her a voice, expressing her suffering, recording this moment for her in my own poetry, crosses my mind. I figure that if left unspoken, this grief—combined with the shortened mourning period for her husband, Uriah—will catch up with her later, and tear us apart.

Then I try to forget all about it. I cannot write her pain. First and foremost I must find a way out of my own.

I try to comfort her, but she seems to be far away, locked in her own grief. I raise her to her feet and carry her—all the way up the long, circular staircase—into my chamber. Kissing her I taste the salt of her tears. I smell the sweet fragrance of her milk.

Then I make love to her.

For me, this is the only way I know to fight off the presence of death. For her, at this moment, the fight is over.

*

Later, lying in bed with my arm around her, her hair across my chest, all is perfectly peaceful, inside and out. For a little while, she forgets her misery. I forget my curse.

I unfurl one of my scrolls, and read to her my latest work, a yet unfinished psalm.

"*Have mercy on me, Oh God, according to your unfailing love. According to your great compassion, blot out my transgressions. Wash away all my iniquity, and cleanse me from my sin.*"

"That," she says, stirring awake all of a sudden, "seems a bit too easy."

I insist, "It took a lot out of me to write these lines."

"Is that what you want, really? A fresh beginning, wiping away all that happened between us? This," she says, "is something I would never pray for, because it takes away the instant, the precious instant when I conceived our child. It takes away his entire existence."

In the face of her resistance I am still determined to go on. "*For I know my transgressions, and my sin is always before me.*"

For her part, she goes on shaking her head.

So I ask, "What?"

"Oh, nothing."

"No really, tell me."

"If only," she says, vaguely.

"What's that supposed to mean?"

"If only you weren't so focused on you alone."

Still eager to impress her I make the mistake of showing her another one of my recent lines, which I find particularly moving. I read aloud, with grand pathos, "*Against you, you only, have I sinned, and done what is evil in your sight, so you are right in your verdict, and justified when you judge.*"

"Not bad," she says.

Then, overcoming a slight hesitation, she turns to me again. "May I ask you something?"

"By all means! Why shouldn't you?

"Is this dedicated to me?"

"Of course not," say I. "This is for the Lord."

At hearing this Bathsheba gets up, gathers her garments, and without another word, she descends down the private staircase, leaving me alone.

Beyond Scandal

Chapter 20

In the wake of my son's death I decide to stop wallowing in sorrow. Instead I must do something about the scandal, because it is quickly getting out of hand. Too many people seem to have nothing better to do than spread rumors, nasty rumors about me. If not handled at once, they may turn into a mob, which is bound to topple me from the throne.

So what choice do I have? I must act, right now. And what a better thing to do than turn their attention to something else, such as our ongoing war against our enemies, the Ammonites. My first in command, Joav, has been fighting against their capital city, Rabbah, for the last two years. Which is not a bad thing, considering it keeps him away from me.

But since the death of Uriah, my people have grown bored with this war, because it is less fun than originally expected. Many of them are weary, and utterly annoyed with news about more wounded, more dead. At this point nothing will set their mind at ease—short of a swift, conclusive victory.

The siege of the city has not come close to a resolution—until now. Here, in my hand, is a new message from Joav, letting me know that at long last, he has managed to capture the royal citadel.

"I've fought against Rabbah and taken its water supply," he writes. "Now muster the rest of the troops and come here. Besiege the city and capture it. Otherwise I'll take the city, and it'll be named after me."

You may think that my general has written this for my sake, because there he is, inviting me to take charge of a war he has been leading mostly on his own, denying himself a victory. But I know him better.

Joav relies on my reluctance to fight, and on my distaste for getting my hands bloody. He would like nothing better than being told, sure! Go ahead already, take the city, and who cares about the name of it. So just to surprise him I do exactly what he has suggested.

I muster the entire army and head out to Rabbah of the children of Ammon. On the way there, as I stand in my chariot, horses flying swifter than wind, I cannot help thinking of that time, that critical moment when I was invited to accompany the king, to ride with his cavalry to my very first battle, not to play before him—but to fight.

"I give you my word, I'll follow you anywhere," I said. "Sounds so exciting, no matter what my mother says."

Saul raised an eyebrow as if to say, I know how you feel. She hides the world from you, doesn't she.

"Yes," I had to agree. "I hate it, hate being protected. Makes me wonder what's on the other side of obedience."

The king paid no attention to what I said. "Listen, boy. Let me tell you one thing: often, when I leave the bloodied scene and ride back here, a long way over the range of the mountains, I don't even realize I've been wounded. My mind wanders, it roams elsewhere... But then, then I look at myself. And what do I see? A slash, deep across my flesh. And this, this is the time—not a moment earlier—when the pain comes. In a snap, it takes a bite."

After that Saul took a long pause, at the end of which he looked straight down at me. "That's how I feel, right this minute," he said. "That's what your music does to me."

*

The walls around the city of Rabbah have already been breached, in one place and another, by the time I get there. Its famished defenders have run out of munitions. They have no arrows left to shoot at us, nor do they have millstones to drop at us from the top of the tower, as we ram their gate with wooden, horned beams.

Faced with barely any resistance I lead my soldiers right up to the gate. The place reeks of despair, and in a strange way I find myself caught up in it.

Before my final attack I find the exact spot where Uriah was shot. Never before have I thought myself gullible enough to believe in spirits, but now here I stand, digging my feet into the bloody soil, daring the shadow of my trusty soldier to reach for me.

At the end of a frenzied hand to hand combat, the king of the Ammonites is brought to his knees before me. I take the crown from his head. It is heavily set with precious stones, I mean, the crown, not the head.

Up to this point I have planned to add it to my collection, and store it upon my return among other crowns, other assorted ornaments in the treasure box, back in my office. But having laid eyes upon this magnificent, sparkling thing I find myself impressed, and decide to make it my own.

It suits me.

I take a great quantity of plunder from the city. As in the past, when I worked in the employ of Achish king of Gath, I find myself reluctant to leave witnesses behind. A complete purge may serve me better.

Nowadays not many recall how, whenever I conquered an area, I made sure to *clean it up*. No historian would dare tell you what exactly that meant, because if they did, I would have to send in my gang and *clean up* after them as well, and they knew all too well not to tempt me to such drastic action. As long as they could see proof of my heavy arm, they went on gagging their own mouth.

My scribe, Nathan, may act sheepish at times—but being a man of God, he has no fear of me. Because of his age, he has made the mistake to stay behind, not realizing that a second-hand report would be marred, unfortunately, with grave inaccuracies. I can only imagine the problem he would have, trying to sort through conflicting stories.

His account would have to be purposely vague, simply to conceal a lack of knowledge. As such, it would translate with opposite meanings into the different languages spoken here, by different people living around our borders, and beyond. I have already seen a number of these translations, two of them coming from as far as Babel.

Here is the first version, describing the collapse of Rabbah and my role in it: "And he brought forth the people that were therein, and put them under saws, and under harrows of iron, and under axes of iron, and made them pass through the brick kiln."

And here, the second: "And he brought out the people who were in it and set them to labor with saws and iron picks and iron axes and made them toil at the brick kilns."

Strange—is it not?—how the introduction of the words '*labor*' and '*toil*' seems to reverse the meaning of this account in such a complete sense, making it palatable, somehow.

Which version is the truth? I will let you decide your own.

*

Having won this decisive victory over the children of Ammon I turn to cross the Jordan river back into our own territory. This is an especially cold, rainy winter day. The sun has been coming close to breaking through the clouds—only to withdraw again. By noon it grows into a steadier shine, but still, gives no warmth. Despite being wrapped in an additional woolen mantel I find myself shivering as I stand there, on the bridge, over the gushing stream. For a moment I reflect on all the soldiers that passed this bridge on their way to the Eastern hills, all the lives lost.

Frothy gray water—dappled with sunlight here and there—is swaying over the river bed, attacking its banks with a sudden burst. The only surface where the stream is completely smooth is right down there, under me. I cast my eyes over it and in a blink I think I catch a reflection. Rising from the deep, there he is: my trusty soldier, Uriah, reaching his willowy arms for me.

Startled I step back. So does he, sinking down deeper. I hop over the bridge and with a swift splash I wade into the water, imagining myself crossing right through his ghost. Perhaps there is a touch, a light touch between us. Or else it is a caress, the slimy caress of underwater plants, wrapping themselves over my limbs.

Dripping wet I mount my horse and ride on.

*

On the way to Bethlehem I pass by a well. It is from here that three of my warriors brought me water when I was a fugitive, hiding in the cave of Adullam. All three of them have perished by now, each one in a different war.

I feel a need to see my father, Jesse, because I know he is getting old. I find him sitting there, by the wayside near Rachel's Tomb, with a downcast, vacant look.

He shows no sign of recognition, and when I quote the first half of his favorite proverb, *"The fathers have eaten sour grapes,"* he just stares at me with dull eyes, instead of completing it with, *"and the children's teeth are set on edge."*

Somewhere along the way, without being aware of it, I have lost my father.

Recalling the scandal I hesitate to go directly back to the palace. Instead I decide to lead the troops elsewhere, any which way. I start traveling around the land, sharing some of my plunder, and talking at great length with my subjects. Only when I sense that I have regained their admiration do I turn back to Jerusalem.

It has been a long journey. I feel it in my bones, as I ride in at the head of a long procession. I smell the familiar fragrance of the soil. An intoxicating smell of Jasmine blooms in the air.

It is spring.

The gleam of a setting sun runs down the curve of my steed's neck, and its mane is flowing around me in the breeze. The horse prances forward, its eagerness matching mine. I lean forward, my skin tingling with excitement.

The riders behind me pull their reins to their stomach, trying to keep the horses from bolting. They do their best to keep their heels down in the stirrups, making them even and heavy so as not to lose their balance. We all know: this is the last bend of the road before we turn into the city gate, before we reach home.

Thinking back about the battle, thinking forward about peace, I know one thing: the destruction of the capital city of the Ammonites could well be the last of my conquests. Gone are the days when I could dare any danger, and emerge unscathed.

War is a young man's game. In encounters to come, taking part in fighting would become increasingly difficult for me.

I remember the stories about our legendary leader, Moses, as he presided over a battle from afar, sitting stiffly on a stone. His brother Aaron on his right, and his companion Hur on his left supported his hands, because they grew heavy with age. Thus his arms were held up steadily until the sun set, which inspired the soldiers to fight, and they overwhelmed their enemy, Amalek, by the edge of the sword.

What can I say but this: I am no Moses. He orchestrated the fight. I have always been right there, in the midst of it.

Let me soften now, let me relax my ambitions. There is no longer a need for me to be torn between being a warrior and being a poet. It is time to relinquish my grip on the sword.

Time to arm myself with the tip of a feather.

Tomorrow I plan to celebrate our arrival, perhaps with a grand parade. It would be accompanied by musicians and dancers. I would honor the living, remember the dead, and bless all of us in glory.

I avoid looking back at my first in command, Joav, who is riding close behind me, and at the rest of the troops, following him. By now I have reached the highest peak. Looking down around me I imagine the sound of shepherds' flutes wafting in the wind, and the blare of trumpets bursting against the slopes, the two strains mixing in and out, out and in, as they rise from the valleys.

For me, this music would mark a departure. Immersing myself in it, no longer would I hear the rasp of a sword, unsheathed. Perhaps the sound I hear is an opening. It is the beginning of harmony in my soul, and of hope for all of us.

*

A short time later, as I ride into the royal courtyard, I see a glow. Torches are burning inside the palace, letting out a flicker here, a flicker there through the windows. They make shadows spill down the stairs from the entrance, in my direction.

And up there, framed against the glitter in the central window, stands a curvy silhouette. Even from a distance, my eyes seek hers. Bathsheba.

I dismount my horse and with measured steps, as befits a king, I go up into the court, which is where I see her taking her seat, right there in the center, among the rest of the women. The first ones to notice my arrival are the boys. They rush to me from all directions, and cling to my hands.

To my amazement my first wife, Michal, and my second, Abigail, kneel before Bathsheba, taking turns rocking something in front of her: a little crib.

She rises to her feet, clasping a hand to her heart. All these months of war, of separation, have collapsed at long last into a single heartbeat.

Bathsheba wipes her eyes, then breathes my name.

To which I say, "Yes, here I am. I have arrived."

"Hush, my love," she whispers. "The baby, he's just fallen asleep."

She can tell, can't she, how surprised I am.

Opening her arms to me she brings me in, which reminds me of the last time I held her. Now as then, her smell is sweet as milk.

This has been an adventurous journey, and a long one. In my exhaustion I can barely move my lips, yet I know she will read me. "What's his name?"

"Solomon."

"Yes," I say, telling myself how fortunate it is for him, and how timely, to be named for peace. "Solomon."

There is a time to kill and a time to heal, a time to tear down and a time to build. How fortunate it is for me to find myself back here. I am a father. I am the keeper of my family, and the shepherd of my people. What a moment this is, the perfect moment to usher in a new era.

Epilogue

Later, when I start awakening from my slumber, the first thing I sense is her touch. Or is it the memory of her touch? I fumble, I reach for it, rolling into the dent in the mattress, which is where she used to lie. I wonder where she is, and why her absence screams at me so crisply, even as I curl myself into the crimson bedspread.

Alas, reality is such a fluid, fleeting thing when you find yourself as old as I am.

Bathsheba is gone, but her voice still echoes in my head. It is still resonating around me in the chamber, whispering softly, "I beg you: show me you still care. Read the scroll. Do it now, David, because this you must realize: my life, and the life of our son, are both in grave danger."

The scroll has been hanging by a thread from Goliath's sword up there over my head, but now it has fallen next to my pillow. With some effort I break the seal. Even so I do not care to read it, or to deal with danger, at my age. She should know that. At his point, the present is such a boring thing for me. Not so the past: I ask myself, over and again, what happened? How in heaven's name did it come to this?

Was it not just yesterday when I was standing there, in my court, beaming a wide smile at the sight of my handsome, mischievous little boys as they came running to me, as they pushed each other aside, simply to cling to my hand?

And didn't Bathsheba raise the baby, then—ever so gently—from his little crib, and let me cradle him in my arms, for the first time? Was it all a dream, nothing more than a yearning for a new beginning?

Was it not then that my wives gathered around me, and we all laughed as they hugged me, hugging them? I remember: I removed the wool mantle from my shoulders, and my fatigue fell away. With renewed vigor I started to relay some of the stories of my long journey, and avoided telling others.

And now, now things have changed. My only daughter, Tamar, is estranged from me. My son Amnon is dead, and so is Absalom. The rest of my children are scheming against me.

The only way they see to remain alive in the midst of all this tumult is by plotting to kill each other, because to them, brotherhood means one thing, and one thing only: an obstacle. Someone to separate them from what they want most, that which they covet with an intensity that is too sick to imagine. The throne.

Of all my many gifts, the only thing they have inherited from me is ambition, which they take to extreme.

Such is my curse, handed down to me many years ago by my scribe, Nathan. With a broken voice I repeat his words, his fateful verdict, "The sword will never depart from your house, because you despised me, and took the wife of Uriah the Hittite to be your own."

I have seen for myself, as every detail has been fleshed out, what exactly he meant when he warned me, "Out of your own household I am going to bring calamity on you. Before your very eyes I will take your wives and give them to one who is close to you, and he will sleep with your wives in broad daylight. You did it in secret, but I will do this thing in broad daylight before all Israel."

Yes, now I know what he meant. I do not care to talk about it. Yet to comfort myself I tend to hide it all, leave it untouched in a special compartment, back there in my mind, which you may call forgetfulness. And then, then I ask myself, where did I go wrong? How, how could I foresee this envy, which is shining sharp between them, like a double-edged sword?

In whose flesh will my lifeblood continue to flow?

How can I prevent my children, even now, from slaying each other, trying to gain something as empty as a crown?

Alas, I am not the only one seeking to understand where I went wrong. My wives are on the case as well, blaming me for the faults of their children, because without a doubt, these innocent souls must have strayed from the straight and narrow for a reason, right?

Clearly it is all my fault. I must have corrupted them. So the only thing that remains to be decided is if it happened because I did not love them enough—or else, because I loved them too much.

How, then, can I leave a legacy behind me? Nothing will remain but glyphs, dead, faded glyphs that no one cares to read, let alone figure out. These marks I made will be left to crumble, crumble into dust inside some discarded papyrus scrolls.

Already I hear my children stealing my words, claiming ownership of my ideas. They do so brazenly, perhaps because they think me deaf to anything they say, anyway.

So the best I can say about them is that they have good taste in helping themselves to my wisdom. But never does it ring true in their mouths, when they say, "*I amassed silver and gold for myself, and the treasure of kings and provinces. I denied myself nothing my eyes desired. I refused my heart no pleasure. Yet when I surveyed all that my hands had done and what I had toiled to achieve, everything was meaningless, a chasing after the wind.*"

*

The two sconces, left and right of the chamber door, still hold the remnants, and the last glimmer of their flames. From time to time, an unsteady glow glances off the blade of Goliath's sword.

I have been lying here, under it, for ages, it seems. Even so, it is going to be a long wait till morning comes. I raise my head from the pillow and set the crown on my head, letting myself feel its weight—and my own vanity—one last time.

It is then that I tell myself that there is a time to be born and a time to die, a time to plant and a time to uproot.

I unfurl the scroll and—without reading what is written in it—I scribble down my own thoughts. With waning strength I prop myself up, trying to catch a glimpse of what lies out there, beyond the sheer curtain that billows, time and again, over the far window. I strain my eyes, trying to detect a shape, a hint of color.

Perhaps, before the edge of the sky starts turning pale, I will raise myself up, somehow. I will sneak out of the palace before the guards wake up, telling no one that I am heading off to a new adventure. This time, what I seek will be entirely different.

It will be redemption.

Before leaving this place I will take off this heavy thing, and let it roll into the corner.

This crown does not define who I am.

I will find my way out, away from here, out the gate and down the stairs, into the courtyard and beyond. There stands my golden chariot. Its design, which is of Hittite origin, is renowned for having four spokes, and for being pulled by a team of horses. Looking at it used to stir me into thinking that one day, when my time comes, I will ascend to heaven in it, leaving a blazing trail of fire beneath its wheels.

That was such a lovely, awe-inspiring thought, especially when combined with another: I used to imagine my trusty soldier, Uriah the Hittite, standing there in the chariot.

I could just see him, waiting for me to step in and take my place by his side before he lifts his whip, cracking it to ignite a sudden flash. Then the horses would bolt into flying away, manes burning, tails flaring amidst a shower of sparks.

On second thought, perhaps this is not such a good idea, considering the excessive heat. I think I will go around the chariot and leave it stuck there, behind me, in the mud.

Along the path I will pass the place where the tent of the Lord is being taken apart, to make room for a permanent, magnificent temple, the likes of which has never been seen in the entire empire. A vision of it is already glittering inside my mind.

Perhaps when it is erected out there, in the real realm—a fine house of cedar—He will forgive me the blood on my hands, which I shed in His name.

I have looked for the best architects in the land and hired them, even approved various parts of their design. So it irks me a bit, knowing that the temple will not be completed in my lifetime, and that credit for constructing it will go to my heir, whoever he may happen to be—but not to me.

Alas, such is vanity! It is, perhaps, the last thing, and the hardest, for me to let go.

Going farther down the hill I will reach the mouth of a cave, just above the Kidron valley. Of their own, my fingers will brush over the texture of its walls. By the damp touch I will recall passing here before, on my way to the water shaft, as I climbed up to storm the city.

I will cradle myself inside one of the stony nooks, and take in the beauty, the eerie beauty of this place, where water gurgles from the deep, from a hidden underground source.

I will imagine myself flowing with it into the valleys, bringing life to faraway fields, to green pastures where young shepherds sleep, where they dream of a life full of peril and excitement. When day comes, one of them will rise, the way I did in my youth. He will start moving the cattle along the wide expanse of land, till dark descends upon the earth.

Later still, at nightfall, I will hear the hoot, the familiar hoot of an owl. Outlined against a dreamy moonlight, it will strike an upright stance, and turn its large, broad head to face me. Again it will repeat its hoot, its song of solitude, which is so akin to mine.

And as it will spread its feathers I will see out there, behind the flutter, a curvaceous outline of a nude. Unable to see the other figures behind her, I will wait for her to come to me. Already I ache to touch her flesh. Her beauty is breathtaking to me. Like a lily among thorns is my darling among the young women.

"Bathsheba," I will whisper, knowing that my voice will be swallowed, it will be lost in the vacuous space.

A moment later, the owl will take off. It will rise away in its silent flight, and the illusive light of the moon will start dimming out.

*

Then, in a blink, I snap back into knowing that I am still lying on my back right here, in my chamber, that I have not made my move yet, and that the sun has just arisen.

I am awakened to all this because of the sound, the familiar footfalls that are approaching my bed. Her fragrance makes me think of the words I wrote for her, long ago, and I whisper them to myself, "*Until the day breaks, and the shadows flee, I will go to the mountain of myrrh, and to the hill of incense...*"

Her name is still trembling on my lips when she draws closer. I bite them and close my eyes, pretending to be asleep.

Bathsheba is followed by my old scribe, Nathan. Lately, he has become her confidant, which puzzles me, because if not for him our first baby would still be alive.

Perhaps I am more vindictive than she is. Perhaps she is willing to set aside her misgivings about the past, because at present she has a better understanding than me of the strife, the political unrest concerning the future of the throne. To advance the chances of her son, Solomon, she has become a master at being devious, and at surrounding herself with dedicated advisors and political allies.

"You must," he tells her. "Really, you must speak to him."

"I tried," she says.

"There's little time left, to turn things around," says Nathan. "The king must take action now, or the two of us, as well as your son, Solomon, are doomed."

"But," she says, dejectedly, "he won't listen to me. Why don't you try?"

"What's the point? If I warn him," says Nathan, "he'll laugh in my face."

"And rightfully so," says Bathsheba. "Wasn't it you—yes, you!—who clouded his head with lofty promises?"

Squirming before her, he says, "I'm sure I don't know what you mean."

At that, she quotes what he told me once, and she does so with surprising precision. "Didn't you tell him, in the name of the Lord Almighty, 'I took you from the pasture, from tending the flock, and appointed you ruler over my people Israel. I have been with you wherever you have gone, and I have cut off all your enemies from before you."

"Yes, I did, but—"

"And, didn't you promise, 'Now I will make your name great, like the names of the greatest men on earth?'"

"Why, was it wrong for me to say that?"

She gives him a look, and says, "Was it ever!"

"Why?"

"Because," she says, "no man felt as invincible as he did, ever since you told him that."

"All I wanted," says Nathan, "was to give him a little nudge, a little bit of confidence."

"Confidence he never lacked," she says, first with a chuckle, then with a sigh. "And didn't you add to that, 'I will provide a place for my people Israel and will plant them so that they can have a home of their own and no longer be disturbed. Wicked people will not oppress them anymore.'"

"You must understand," he says. "This particular vision is slower to happen than others."

She rolls her eyes in disbelief. "In this case," she says, "don't call it a *prophesy*. Call it simply a *dream*."

"*Prophesy* sounds bigger," he says, "and more promising. I like to leave some impression."

"Worst of all," she says, "didn't you tell David, 'When your days are over and you rest with your ancestors, I will raise up your offspring to succeed you, your own flesh and blood, and I will establish your kingdom?'"

To which Nathan says, "I was a bit vague there, wasn't I?"

And Bathsheba says, "You need to ask? Of course you were!"

To which she adds, "That goes directly to the question, who that offspring might be. It goes to the question who, in this place, will live, and who will die, before this day is over."

He bows his head, with a sudden shiver.

Meanwhile, she leans over my pillow, so close that I hear strings of jewels dancing around her neck, and catch a glimpse of her earring of gold, studded with silver. She picks up the scroll, over which I have scribbled my thoughts, just a little while ago.

"Well?" says Nathan. "Has he broken the seal? Has he read my warning?"

"The seal," she says, "has been broken. Wait, there's something else."

He stands there patiently, to hear what she has to say.

Under the crimson blanket I cannot help but shake my head at the notion that she has to have the last word—but even so, I am glad that she chooses it to be mine:

I cannot see her face, but by her voice I know that she is awash with tears, as she reads my words aloud, "*Lord, do not rebuke me in your anger, or discipline me in your wrath. Have mercy on me, Lord, for I am faint. Heal me, Lord, for my bones are in agony. My soul is in deep anguish.*"

How long, Lord, how long?

To be continued with:

THE DAVID CHRONICLES
Volume III

The Edge of Revolt

About this Book

When Bathsheba becomes pregnant, David attempts to cover up the ensuing scandal. He sends her husband, Uriah—who serves him faithfully in his army—to his death. And for the rest of his life, David is tormented by the memory of that moment. Will their forbidden love undo his entire legacy? Can he muster the strength to keep his promise to her and protect their son from danger? Will he find redemption?

This is volume II of the trilogy The David Chronicles, told candidly by the king himself. David uses modern language, indicating that this is no fairytale. Rather, it is a story that is happening here and now. Listen to his voice as he undergoes a profound change, realizing the curse looming over his entire future.

If you like middle eastern historical romance and forbidden love affair, this King David novel has a modern twist like no book you have read before, bringing King David of the bible to life against the background of Israel historical fiction. With vivid descriptions of court intrigue, it paints King David biography in a way that is both classic and timely.

About the Author

Uvi Poznansky is a *USA TODAY* bestselling, award-winning author, poet and artist. "I paint with my pen," she says, "and write with my paintbrush." Her romance boxed set, A Touch of Passion, was the 2016 winner of The Romance Reviews Readers' Choice Awards. Her romantic suspense boxed set, Love Under Fire, reached #44 on the *USA TODAY* bestselling list.

She earned her B. A. in Architecture and Town Planning from the Technion in Haifa, Israel. During her studies and in the years immediately following her graduation, she practiced with an innovative Architectural firm, taking part in the design of a large-scale project, *Home for the Soldier*.

Having moved to Troy, N.Y. with her husband and two children, Uvi received a Fellowship grant and a Teaching Assistantship from the Architecture department at Rensselaer Polytechnic Institute. There, she guided teams in a variety of design projects and earned her M.A. in Architecture. Then, taking a sharp turn in her education, she earned her M.S. degree in Computer Science from the University of Michigan.

During the years she spent in advancing her career—first as an architect, and later as a software engineer, software team leader, software manager and a software consultant (with an emphasis on user interface for medical instruments devices)—she wrote and painted constantly. In addition, she taught art appreciation classes.

Her versatile body of work can be seen on her blog, which includes poems, short stories, bronze and ceramic sculptures, paper engineering projects, oil and watercolor paintings, charcoal, pen and pencil drawings, and mixed media. In addition, she posts her thoughts about the creative process, excerpts from her writing, reader reviews, and author interviews. She engages readers and writers in conversation on her Goodreads group, The Creative Spark.

Uvi published a poetry book in collaboration with her father, Zeev Kachel. Later she published two children's books, *Jess and Wiggle* and *Now I Am Paper*, which she illustrated, and for which she created animations. You can find these animations on her Goodreads author page.

Coma Confidential and *Virtually Lace* are volume I and II of Ash Suspense Thrillers with a Dash of Romance, featuring a young software engineer, Michael, and his sweetheart, Ash. With each new case, they combine his methodical computer simulation of events with her spark of intuition to solve the crime.

My Own Voice, *The White Piano* (woven together in *Apart from Love*), *The Music of Us,* and *Dancing with Air* are volume I, II, III and IV of *Still Life with Memories,* a family saga with love stories that develop in the face of hardship and illness over two generations, starting at the beginning of WWII with Lenny, a soldier, and Natasha, a rising star.

Rise to Power, *A Peek at Bathsheba*, and *The Edge of Revolt* are volume I, II, and III of *The David Chronicles*, telling the story of David as you have never heard it before: from the king himself, telling the unofficial version, the one he never allowed his court scribes to recount. In his mind, history is written to praise the victorious—but at the last stretch of his illustrious life, he feels an irresistible urge to tell the truth.

A Favorite Son, her novella, is a new-age twist on an old yarn. It is inspired by the biblical story of Jacob and his mother Rebecca, plotting together against the elderly father Isaac, who is lying on his deathbed. This is no old fairy tale. Its power is here and now, in each one of us.

Twisted is a unique collection of tales. In it, the author brings together diverse tales, laden with shades of mystery. Here, you will come into a dark, strange world, a hyper-reality where nearly everything is firmly rooted in the familiar—except for some quirky detail that twists the yarn, and takes it for a spin in an unexpected direction.

Home, her deeply moving poetry book in tribute of her father, includes her poetry and prose, as well as translated poems from the pen of her father, the poet and author Zeev Kachel.

Most of these books are available in all three editions: ebook, audio, and print.

About the Cover

My book, *A Peek at Bathsheba*, includes a sighting of Bathsheba at the mouth of a cave, located just above the Kidron valley, near Jerusalem. The setting immediately brought to my mind *A Woman Bathing in a Stream*, painted in 1655 by Rembrandt, immediately after he painted *Bathsheba at Her Bath*.

During the history of art, most artists portrayed Bathsheba as a fleshy, mature woman. They often placed her in a lush outdoor scenery, such as a royal garden, with flowing water or with a fountain. Spotting a forbidden woman in a setting reminiscent of the Garden of Eden is a tempting fantasy, and quite a departure from the biblical account, that states she was bathing on her roof. Artists go after their own heart—and so, indeed, do writers—to suggest the emotional essence of the story.

Rembrandt places his figure not in a garden, but in a cave with a pool of water, which is at once an outdoor and indoor scene (and in *Bathsheba at Her Bath* he presented her in an indoor scene, in her bedroom.)

Unlike paintings done by other artists—depicting Susanna and the Elders, Bathsheba, or the goddess Diana, who were all spied upon while bathing—this painting does not show the peeping man. Instead, Rembrandt supplants him by you, the viewer. Also, the woman in his painting is in control of the situation, rather than a victim of it.

Rembrandt worked mostly with a grays, browns, and blacks, setting objects back by plunging them into this dark tone, and bringing them forward by shining a bright light directly upon them, creating stark contrasts. The resulting image is sculptural in nature, and strikingly dramatic.

Clearly, the composition of my watercolor painting is inspired by his admirable art, shares a similar spirit of intimacy, and maintains a loving respect for the model. Here is my approach, my homage to it, which illuminates the new vision I use for the story.

I strive to maintain a sculptural feel for Bathsheba, but take the freedom to play with a splash of colors, so as to draw contrasts between cool and warm hues. I create a variety of textures, using a loose, spontaneous brushstroke. This I achieve by applying puddles of pigments over Yupo paper, which (unlike traditional watercolor paper) is non-absorbent. I let these puddles drip in some places, and in other places, I lift and shape them into careful designs, using various tools.

The font selected for the title depicts a regal, dynamically slanted, and rather grandiose handwriting style, just the way I imagine David's penmanship in his private diary.

By contrast to the title, the font selected for the name of the trilogy —*The David Chronicles*—is a more formal one, and it is presented in capitals. This adheres to the font scheme for the cover of the first volume, *Rise to Power*.

At the top, the letters are bathed in golden light, which fades gradually towards the bottom. Down there, they are soaked in a blood red color, as befits this dramatic affair of love and war.

A Peek at Bathsheba is one volume out of a trilogy. Therefore I am designing the spines of all three covers to have a matching feel in terms of the image and font scheme. So when you place them on your bookshelf, one spine next to the other, all three volumes will visually belong together. Together they will grace the look of your library.

A Note to the Reader

Thank you for reading this book! I hope you enjoyed it. If you did, I invite you to check out more books from the same pen. There is always a new project on my drawing board, so come back to check it out.

I would love to hear what you thought of this book. You have the power of bringing it to the attention of more readers, by posting your own review. It would mean so much to me.

And another thing you can do to help me spread the word is this: please tell your friends about my work. How else will they hear about the story? How else will the characters, who sprang from my mind onto these pages, leap from there into new minds?

Bonus Excerpts

Excerpt: Rise to Power

To show respect I fall to my knees before him. The floor is cold, having absorbed the damp of a long winter. The surface is porous, even crumbly here and there, cut of rocks from the Judea mountains. So is the surface of the stage, right in front of my eyes.

I cannot help noting the marks drawn by his spear in the film of dirt up there, around his boots. Scratch, twist, scratch again... No wonder he seems to be in such a royal pain: with all these attendants here to serve him, not a single one has managed to come up with the bright idea of sweeping the floor. They all carry weapons, but not one has a broom.

Sitting nearly immobile, Saul seems as chalky as the walls around him. He sits crumpled—in an odd way—upon the throne. His nails keep digging into the little velvety cushions that are stretched over the carved armrests. Not once does he give a nod in my direction, nor does he acknowledge my presence in any other way.

Which agitates me. It awakens my doubt, doubt in my skill. Much the same as I feel in my father's presence. Repressed. On the verge of acting out.

So, rising to my feet I blurt out, "Your majesty—"

"Don't talk," whispers one of the attendants. "Play."

I am pushed a step or two backwards, so as to maintain proper distance from the presence of the king. My name is called out in a clunky manner of introduction, after which I am instructed to choose from an array of musical instruments. I figure they must be the loot of war. So when I play them, the music of enemy tribes shall resound here, around the hall.

I pluck the strings of a sitar, then put it back down and pick up a lyre, which I make quiver, quiver with notes of fire! Then I rap, clap, tap, snap my fingers, and just to be cute, play a tune on my flute, after which I do a skip, skip, skip and a back flip.

It is a long performance, and towards the end of it I find myself trying to catch my breath. Alas, my time is up. Even so I would not stop.

Entranced I go on to recite several of my poems, which I have never done before, for fear of exposing my most intimate, raw emotions, which is a risky thing for a man, and even riskier for a boy my age. Allowing your vulnerability to show takes one thing above all: a special kind of courage. Trust me, it takes balls.

So, having read the last verse I cast a look at the attendants, especially the ones closest to me. Their faces seem to have softened. I can sense them beginning to adore me. One of them comes over and taps my shoulder, which nearly knocks me off my feet. Another one laughs. Others wipe their eyes.

Then I glance at Saul, hoping for a tear, a smile, a word of encouragement. Instead I note an odd, vacant look on his face. Utter indifference. It stings me. Am I too short, too young, too curly for the role he has in mind for me?

Wiping the sweat off my brow I bow down before him and turn to leave the court, which is the moment he leans forward on his spear.

"Stop right there," says Saul. "Tell me: what can you do best?"

To which I say, "Recover."
He glowers at me as if to ask, Recover? From what?
"From this," I point out, daring to be honest. "Rejection."

Excerpt: The Edge of Revolt

At last, "Decisive action may be easy for a king," I tell her. "But as a father I must weigh every word I speak, because in the future it may leave a scar upon the hearts of my children."

Somewhat reluctantly she says, "I understand."

"I hope you do," say I. "They are, all of them, my flesh and blood."

"Then, act as a king," she says. "Not as a father. Name the one who will succeed you, the one who—in your judgement—may become a better ruler than the others."

I have to admit, "I have yet to make up my mind," which fills her eyes with worry. She knows all too well that Solomon, being the younger son, has less of a change to win my favor.

"Decide," she says. "And make your wishes known. That in itself may bring about a change, a peaceful transition of power. Otherwise, I'm afraid there will be mayhem. It will start at sunrise."

I let go of her hand, because to say my next sentence I must not lean on anyone.

But before I can muster my pride, and take air in my lungs, and clear my throat to state, in my most regal tones, "I am still the king, am I not," I find myself staggering. In the next instant, there I am, a heap of arms and legs spilled on the floor, twisting in agony from the sudden chill overtaking me.

I reach up, trying to breathe her name. And I wonder what this suffering may look like, to her and to a heavenly city watching over me, floating silent and forlorn on the hill.

Overhead, a cloud breaks off from the others and moves in a new direction. Its wooly, dim grays are drifting across. I squint, rub my eyes. Now, in a separate layer, another image starts floating past: the way she looked, right here on this roof, when we came out of these doors the very first time.

I remember: scattered petals flew off, swirling in the glow around her long, silky hair that started cascading under her, onto the tile floor. In the background, a vine of roses twisted over the wooden lattice and into it. Between its diagonal slats I saw a diamond here, a diamond there of the heavens. I wondered then about the black void that was gaping upon us, dotted by a magical glint of starlight.

Separated from her by the thought of a kiss I sensed her heat, and the gust of air, which was sweetly scented by roses and by her flesh—but I could not tell if the breath between us was hers or mine. Which is when I knew, for the first time in my life, that she would always be part of my essence. I would be part of hers.

Accidentally the goblet, which she had set down next to her, tipped over and some of the wine spilled over her hip. The crisp sound of breaking glass rang in my ear. It marked the moment, from which I could not turn back. Never would I be able to put it out of my mind.

Yes, this was my fault: taking a woman that belonged to another. Soon after came the blunder: bringing her husband, Uriah, back from the front, that he may sleep with her, which would have explained her pregnancy ever so conveniently.

And when that did not go as planned, then came another mistake, the worst of all: sending him back to the battlefield, with my sealed letter in hand, arranging for his death.

All the while, my boys were learning their own lessons—not from my psalms but from my deeds. One error begets another, each one bringing a new calamity over me, over my family, and over this entire land. Sin followed by execution, followed by revolt, escape, execution, revolt...

Had I known back then the results of the results of my mistake, the curse looming over my life ever since that time, would I still choose to do it?

Bathsheba tries to raise me to my feet. Her fragrance brings back to me the sunny, warm hues of spring. The fears, the doubts flee away when we are that close. I adore the way she calls my name, the way she sighs. With every sweet word I fall deeper into her eyes.

How can love be a mistake? In my passion for her—then as now—what choice do I have?

I want to tell her, "Let me close my eyes. Let me remember."

Excerpt: The Music of Us

My son, Ben, has been gone for a month now, staying in some youth hostel in Rome. If I call him, if I stumble into revealing how scared I am that his mother is losing her mind, he may listen. He may heed my fears, grudgingly, and come back here, not even knowing how to offer his support to me. Should I ask for it? The last thing I wish to do is lean on him for help. He is not strong enough, and whatever the problem may be with her, I can grit my teeth and handle it, somehow, all by myself. Besides, I pray for a spontaneous change in her. I mean, her memory may take a turn for the better just as quickly as it has deteriorated.

Given this hope I decide that for now I will not schedule the head X-Ray that her doctor recommended for her. I figure she has been through so many checkups, so many exams to rule out depression, vitamin B deficiency, and a long list of other possible ailments, all of which has been in vain.

So far, the results have failed to produce a conclusive diagnosis, and this new X-Ray will be no different, because from what I have read, Alzheimer's disease can be determined only through autopsy, by linking clinical measures with an examination of brain tissue. So this new medical hypothesis is just that: a hypothesis. One that cannot be proven; one that cannot go away. An ever-present threat.

Perhaps all she needs is rest. Time, I tell myself. I must give her time. Meanwhile I resolve to keep her condition secret from everyone, especially from my son. Let him enjoy his time away from home, his independence.

Since his departure I called him only once, three weeks ago, and said little, except for blurting out the mundane, "How's Rome?"

"Great," he said vaguely, adding no particulars.

I could not help myself from asking. "So, what about your plans?"

"What about them?"

"D'you have any?"

"For now I have none," he admitted, and immediately changed the subject. "How's mom?"

"Fine."

"Is she?"

"She is," I lied, hoping that the sound of my voice would not betray the tensing of my muscles, the tightening of my jaws.

"Oh good," he said. "Really, really good."

There is only one thing more difficult than talking to Ben, and that is writing to him. Amazingly, having to conceal what his mother is going through makes every word—even on subjects unrelated to her—that much harder. I find myself oppressed by my own self-imposed discipline, the discipline of silence.

And what can I tell him, really? That I keep digging into the past, mining its moments, trying to piece them together this way and that, dusting off each memory of Natasha, of how we were, the highs and lows of the music of us, to find out where the problem may have started?

To him, that may seem like an exercise in futility. For me, it is a necessary process of discovery, one that is as tormenting as it is delightful. If the dissonance in our life would fade away, so will the harmony.

Sometimes I go as far back as the moment we first met, when I was a soldier and she—a star, brilliant yet illusive. Natasha was a riddle to me then, and to this day, with all the changes she has gone through, she still is.

I often wonder: can we ever understand, truly understand each other—soldier and musician, man and woman, one heart and another? Will we ever again dance together to the same beat? Is there a point where we may still touch?

Excerpt: Marriage before Death

Without uttering a sound I gave her a look, begging her to leave. Rochelle gave one to me, begging me to play along.

Out loud she said, "Oh how I hate you! I hate you now more than I ever loved you!"

At that, the SS officer burst out laughing. It lasted quite a while, or so it seemed to me, and by the time it finally ended, a cruel smile was left across his face, stretching from one pointy ear to the other.

"*Ach*," he hissed. "What a woman! Cold one minute—hot the next!"

Rochelle hung her eyes on me one more time.

"At the very least," she implored, "you should say you are sorry, so sorry to have left me in such a difficult situation!"

The SS officer cut in.

"Didn't I tell you?" he asked her. "His kind, they have no morals! Worse than animals is what they are."

She turned away and went back to his side. From there she said, in a tone of regret, "Right you are. I was naive, up to now, to hope for anything different from him."

Over her sorrow, the SS officer went on to say, "How could you ever let yourself be seduced by such a man?"

She shook her head. "How silly of me! How foolish it is to hope! I was sure he would confirm to everyone here his desire to marry me."

To which the SS officer said, "Now, mademoiselle, you have learned your lesson."

She gave him a tearful smile, but then could not help crying out to me, "Oh, for heaven's sake, don't you get it? I'm expecting your child!"

At that I had a change of heart. Why? First, because I was moved to tears by her plea, no matter if it was a fake one or not; and second, because what had I got to lose?

So I uttered, "Forgive me, Rochelle."

"What?" she asked. "What did you say?"

"Forgive me," I said, with a catch in my throat. "If I were a free man I would gladly keep my promise to you."

A triumphant smile played on her red lips. Yet, for just a moment, she was silent.

I thought she might make peace with me, now that I relented. Instead, she turned to the SS officer.

"Herr Müller," she said. "I'm not here to beg for mercy for this man."

In surprise, "You're not?" he asked, raising a thick eyebrow.

And from the other side of the table, his French collaborator echoed, "You're not?"

My face was still burning, still stinging from that slap of hers. I bit my lips to overcome the pain. If I could muster the nerve to speak up once more, I would ask her the very same thing.

Really? You're not?

"No," she stressed.

The toothbrush mustache under Herr Müller's nose started to twitch. Perhaps he was becoming suspicious of her.

"I thought," he said, "that you had a big favor to ask of me."

And she said, "I do."

And he said, “Well? What is it, then?”

“For the sake of my family,” said Rochelle, “for the pride of my father, for my own honor, and for the future of this baby, I cannot be an unwed mother! I’d rather die!”

Becoming somewhat impatient, “*Ach!*” he said. “You should have thought of that earlier, before you got involved with the likes of him.”

It was then that she said, “I promise, Herr Müller, giving me what I ask for is sure to give you the greatest pleasure, because it is just what this man deserves.”

“Which is what?”

“Marriage before death.”

Books by Uviart

Coma Confidential

(Volume I of *Ash Suspense Thrillers with a Dash of Romance*)

Paperback: 978-1791691592 Kindle: B07L92YHST

Audiobook US: soon... UK: soon...

Audible: soon... iTunes: soon..

Virtually Lace

(Volume II of *Ash Suspense Thrillers with a Dash of Romance*)

Paperback: 978-1790407187 Kindle: B07L968RXD

Audiobook US: soon... UK: soon...

Audible: soon... iTunes: soon...

My Own Voice

(Volume I of *Still Life with Memories*)

Paperback: 978-0-9849932-1-5 Kindle: B013TA3FBS

Audiobook US: B015F0CU2U UK: B015DB5V5O

Audible: B015DAVRWQ iTunes: id1040237919

The White Piano

(Volume II of *Still Life with Memories*)

Paperback: 978-1517049447 Kindle: B013TAU7L4

Audiobook US: B015F0CL06 UK: B015D7JOJ2

Audible: B015D7G5VW iTunes: id1040238378

The Music of Us

(Volume III of *Still Life with Memories*)

Paperback: 978-0-9849932-9-1 Kindle: B013TCYWHC

Audiobook US: B01A635Y10 UK: B01A6369QE

Audible: B01A640PLS iTunes: id1072442964

Dancing with Air

(Volume IV of *Still Life with Memories*)

Paperback: 978-1536896534 Kindle: B01I4ENROY

Audiobook US: B01N2QZBY9 UK: B01MSW6OVE

Audible: B01MTXPW5G iTunes: id1184500169

Marriage before Death

(Volume V of *Still Life with Memories*)

Paperback: 978-1974001736 Kindle: B0746NW5CD

Audiobook US: B0778T7B6H UK: B0778W3GYV

Audible: B0778SWSXF iTunes: id1318734393

Apart from Love

(Still Life with Memories Bundle I)

Paperback: 978-0-9849932-0-8 Kindle: B006WPITP0

Audiobook US: B00D1YLITY UK: B00CZDFI7A

Audible: B00CME0G2E iTunes: id653509873

Apart from War

(Still Life with Memories Bundle II)

Paperback: 978-1792131592 Kindle: B07MMZLD7Z

Audiobook US: Soon UK: Soon

Audible: Soon iTunes: Soon

Rise to Power

(Volume I of *The David Chronicles*)

Paperback: 978-0-9849932-4-6 Kindle: B00H6PMZ0U

Audiobook US: B00IP4I08W UK: B00IOE266U

Audible: B00IO3NAIY iTunes: id833594014

A Peek at Bathsheba

(Volume II of *The David Chronicles*)

Paperback: 978-0-9849932-7-7 Kindle: B00LEPPDV6

Audiobook US: B00PMA8NS4 UK: B00PKJMZFE

Audible: B00PKG8K4W iTunes: id941881557

The Edge of Revolt

(Art book. Volume III of *The David Chronicles*)

Paperback: 978-0984993284 Kindle: B00Q5WVKA6

Audiobook US: B0711P6GJK UK: B0716VKVF9

Audible: B0716VKVP6 iTunes: id1237371808

Inspired by Art: Fighting Goliath

(Art book. Volume IV of *The David Chronicles*)

Kindle: B01MSBNSE4

Inspired by Art: Fall of a Giant

(Art book. Volume V of *The David Chronicles*)

Kindle: B01MSBS82Q

Inspired by Art: Rise to Power

(Art book. Volume VI of *The David Chronicles*)

Kindle: B01N2786VX

Inspired by Art: A Peek at Bathsheba

(Art book. Volume VII of *The David Chronicles*)

Kindle: B01MUFS9OA

Inspired by Art: The Edge of Revolt

(Art book. Volume VIII of *The David Chronicles*)

Kindle: B01N6ZG0W8

Inspired by Art: The Last Concubine

(Art book. Volume IX of *The David Chronicles*)

Kindle: B01N2AXQP2

The David Chronicles

(Volume I, II, and III)

Kindle: B00QYGF6WG

A Favorite Son

Paperback: 978-0-9849932-5-3 Kindle: B00AUZ3LGU

Audiobook US: B00C43RHRU UK: B00C48A4YI

Audible: B00C3JVLZO iTunes: id630292672

Twisted

Paperback: 978-0984993260 Kindle: B00D7Q3IY4

Nook: 2940151689588 Apple: id958710948

Kobo: 9781507018101

Audiobook US: B00EFCOMM6 UK: B00EFQJJZC

Audible: B00EEG4DNQ iTunes: id686672397

Home

Paperback: 978-09849932-3-9 Kindle: B00960TE3Y

Nook: 2940151729468 Apple: id958855135

Kobo: 9781507045688

Audiobook US B00EQ0II3Q UK: B00EPKKBO6

Audible: B00EPHL15C

בית

(Poetry in Hebrew)
Paperback: 978-1494920968

Nook: 1127367962 Apple: id1302908918

Kobo: 9781540199966

Children's Books by Uviart

Jess and Wiggle

Paperback: 978-1494920968 Kindle: B013D1W0SM

Now I Am Paper

Paperback: 978-1494919429 Kindle: B00YQS4O72

Made in the USA
Lexington, KY
18 January 2019